Girl Under the Ice

An Ella Porter Mystery Thriller
Book 1

Georgia Wagner

Text Copyright © 2022 Georgia Wagner

Publisher: Greenfield Press Ltd

The right of Georgia Wagner to be identified as author of the Work has been asserted in accordance with the Copyright, Designs and Patents Act 1988

All rights reserved.

The book is copyright material and must not be copied, reproduced, transferred, distributed, leased, licensed or publicly performed or used in any way except as specifically permitted in writing by the publishers, as allowed under the terms and conditions under which it was purchased or as strictly permitted by applicable copyright law. Any unauthorised distribution or use of this text may be a direct infringement of the author's and publisher's rights and those responsible may be liable in law accordingly.

'Girl Under the Ice' is a work of fiction. Names, characters, businesses, organisations, places, events, and incidents either are the product of the author's imagination or are used fictitiously. Any resemblance to actual persons, living or dead, and events or locations is entirely coincidental.

Contents

1.	Prologue	1
2.	Chapter 1	8
3.	Chapter 2	24
4.	Chapter 3	40
5.	Chapter 4	50
6.	Chapter 5	57
7.	Chapter 6	66
8.	Chapter 7	70
9.	Chapter 8	77
10.	Chapter 9	93
11.	Chapter 10	104
12.	Chapter 11	110
13.	Chapter 12	117

14. Chapter 13   124

15. Chapter 14   142

16. Chapter 15   150

17. Chapter 16   161

18. Chapter 17   166

19. Chapter 18   178

20. Chapter 19   193

21. Chapter 20   206

22. Chapter 21   221

23. Chapter 22   226

24. What is Next for Ella Porter   240

25. Other Books by Georgia Wagner   242

26. Also by Georgia Wagner   244

27. Want to know more?   246

28. About the Author   248.

PROLOGUE

BENEATH A FROSTED SEA, under five inches of ice that gave a ghostly, bluish glow, small bursts of bubbles erupted past Janice Longstreet's scuba mask. Five hours into her dive, Janice double-checked her oxygen gauge, her breathing steady, her motions controlled in a way that hinted at her status as a veteran diver.

She paused again, glancing up and watching the source of her initial distraction. A dark figure moving on the ice, far above. Little more than a shadow against the crystal veneer covering the sea. She frowned as the shadow moved in the direction of the dredge and the small, snowbound, gold-mining tent.

She checked her radio, and said, "Baron, is that you?"

A pause, a deep breath, then another burst of bubbles. Then a voice in her ear, "What was that, Jan?"

"No, we're good," she said. "Just checking you're there." She watched the ice again. The shadow was gone. She supposed her guy-in-the-chair had needed to go turn some snow yellow. Still, she would've preferred if he'd let her know he was taking a break. Then again, five hours was a long time to hold it, watching her oxygen, her hot water, the sluice box... In Janice's opinion, diving was far preferable to the chair above.

For some, a five-hour underwater dive in the heart of the freezing water would have proven too frightening. The solitude. The cold. The threat of hypothermia, of anything prickly or toothy lurking along the Alaskan sea beds. But for someone like Janice, this was her happy place.

And what *made* it happy was the gleaming glints sucked into the hose between her gloved hands. She watched as the pieces of gold were consumed by the large, ten-inch nozzle. She kicked, propelling herself forward, dragging the gold-mining nozzle further along the bottom of the sea.

Some claimed that Nome was the largest gold-pan in the world. Janice didn't know about any of that—all she did was spend time on the box. The sluice box, which was visible twenty feet above her, spat the trailings, the mud, the filth, back into the water. The gold was caught in the box, since it was heavier than the sediment. A long hose stretched from the dredge above her, where it rested on top of the ice.

She kept track of the opening in the ice far above, which was outlined with small blue flares in order to help her locate it from the turbid depths. Any diver's worst nightmare, when swimming under thousands of tons of ice, was rising in the wrong spot while low on oxygen, bumping one's head against the ice, only to realize the lines were tangled.

To drown in the icy Bering Sea, trapped under the ice, in the dark only inches away from precious air... It was enough to chill the bones.

And yet, Janice had done *eight* hour dives before in the same black diver's suit she currently wore. Diligently and determinedly sucking up the gold dust off the bottom of the ocean floor. Her husband had made something of a name for himself as a gold miner in Nome, and she was his secret weapon.

Janice didn't care for the spotlight. She didn't even spend much of the money earned from the sale of the gold. To her, she had the fever, as some called it. The insatiable desire to find *more* without thought to why. It was her obsession, and it kept her in the cold water.

Suddenly, the faint buzz of the constantly open radio channel in her ears went quiet. She frowned, glancing up again at the ice. "Hey Baron, you there?" she said. No response. "Hey!" she said, louder. No reply.

She sighed. He must've hit the mute by accident. She was going to have to tell her husband that the rookie just wasn't cut out for this sort of thing. He'd forgotten the generator two weeks before then, last week, had dropped the small, portable pump into a puddle of salt water.

Protocol dictated she ought to return to the surface. But they were on a paystreak... She huffed in frustration, then counted down in her head. Sixty more seconds, then she'd go topside, above the ice, and give her would-be assistant what-for.

She shifted the hose, moving towards a more gravelly patch of earth. She watched as a small nugget, the size of her pinkie finger, sucked up the hose. Good pay dirt, this. They'd paid nearly five million dollars to lease these thousand acres off the coast. It would take them months to recoup their losses, but her husband, Vince Longstreet, had been convinced it was a good investment.

Her hose suddenly bumped against something, and Janice frowned. She tried to tug on the hose, but the metal lip of the ten-inch nozzle tapped against something in the muddy sentiment. She tried to readjust, but the metal lip was hooked. She frowned, reaching with her gloved hand towards—

A sudden powerful force sucked her hand up the nozzle.

Her heart jumped into her throat, and she yelped behind her scuba mask. More bubbles erupted around her. Her skin went cold, even though hot water was being pumped continually through her diving suit.

She managed to twist her hand to present as small of a surface area as possible and then pulled, with great effort, her fist from inside the nozzle, panting a bit as she did it. She hovered in the water at the bottom of the sea, straddling the thick hose and holding to the nozzle for guidance.

"Hey, you there?" she tried the radio again. Still nothing. Was he taking another break?

She frowned, beginning to turn, to head back to the surface, but then something caught her eye. She went still, frowning at the sediment. Normally, the silt and mud needed to be removed to reveal a more gravelly substance, or black sand—the thicker sediments which hinted at gold.

But here, in this section of the underwater sand bank, she found herself staring at churned gravel. Someone had already been through here...

That wasn't right. The lease said this hadn't been mined in years.

She stared at the item her hose had caught on. And now a slow chill that had nothing to do with the temperature prickled down her spine.

The dead quiet of the radio silence in her scuba mask took on a far more ominous veneer. As she stared at the protruding item from the gravel, she realized there was no one to hear her scream.

But her breathing came rapidly now, her stomach twisting. She was hyperventilating and wasn't sure how to stop.

Her eyes were the size of saucers behind her glass mask. As more bubbles burst from her mouthpiece, erupting up, she stared at a jutting, pale branch emerging from the ground.

Except, branches didn't have skeletal hands.

Nor were they attached to a shoulder bone... a rib cage visible now. The more sediment the hose sucked up, the more of the skeleton was revealed. "Turn off the hose—turn it off!" she was shouting in her mask.

But nothing happened. And then something *clicked.* She felt a sudden shift in her suit. The flow of hot water had been severed.

Now panic filled her. A second later...

The oxygen went. For such long dives, the efficacy of scuba tanks would have been threatened, so oxygen was pumped from the surface tanks through the hose line.

But now... she couldn't breathe. She was inhaling, but nothing entered her lungs.

Someone was shutting things down above the water.

A skeletal face leered from the mud where the sediment was continually ripped away. And then a second skeletal face... Bodies. More than one. She'd found an underwater burial site.

And someone was shutting down her oxygen.

She heard a splash, and as she tried to disentangle from the hose, kicking away, she turned to look. A body in the water above her, floating face up, red ribbons of blood spreading around him... She recognized her assistant's thick, wool coat.

Baron didn't move, lying dead, floating in the opening she was heading towards. Her eyes bugged. And now she spotted a shadow moving on the ice again. Not her assistant. Someone else. *Something* else.

She couldn't breathe. Was freezing now. Hypothermia could set in within seconds in these freezing temperatures. But corpses in the ground behind her. A body above her. Panic filled her. She wanted to stay down here, on the ocean floor, where she felt safe. The gold still glinted in the sediment, but what had seemed so important only moments before was of absolutely no concern to her now. Some things were far more valuable than gold fever.

Another splash.

Another diver. A figure in scuba gear was slipping past the body, moving through the opening in the ice.

Her eyes bugged as the diver moved straight towards her. Something glinted in his hand.

A small ice pick, brandished like a weapon. A thin trail of red ink fluttered in ribbons from the pick. And the dark figure in the scuba mask swam directly at her, bubbles streaming past his mask.

And now she did scream.

And as she'd guessed, not a soul could hear her.

CHAPTER 1

ELLA WRINKLED HER NOSE as sea spray dappled the cracked window near the captain's tattooed arm. The boat skipped across the water, carrying her towards the icebound city of Nome.

"Dangerous straits, these," the captain said in his nearly indeterminable accent. A combination of Canadian, a speech impediment and the bottle of whiskey he kept hidden under the steering wheel of the small cargo vessel.

Ella nodded absentmindedly, watching as a chunk of ice floated past. Ahead, she spotted her new post. The field office in Nome, Alaska, was responsible for some three-thousand year-round residents who lived on the coast of the Bering Sea.

Multiple rings of ice spread out from the shoreline, encasing the water beneath the crystal shield. The circles of thick frost over the sea looked like pure vanilla icing on a cake.

"Ever been before?" the captain asked, glancing at her. His breath smelled faintly of cigarette smoke. Ella, however, smiled politely. She didn't step back, she simply weathered the storm of his breath.

No need to offend the old sea-dog over something so small as bad breath. She'd made a career for herself by putting her own wants and desires on the back burner. Catering to the emotional needs of others. Avoiding offending anyone. And now, after a meteoric rise back in Quantico, the FBI agent had been exiled to this frozen wilderness.

She peered across the flat land—very few trees visible. The mountains behind Nome touched the sky, also burdened with snow. During the summer, the mountains and surrounding flatland would shed the snowy burden, bursting with scrubby vegetation and redolent mountain flowers.

But now, she found herself zipping across the sea towards a winter wonderland. She'd chartered the boat specially. Normally, during such conditions, planes would be taken to Nome, rather than small cargo vessels.

But the only planes currently being run that stopped in Nome were owned by Porter Enterprises.

The Porter family had deep roots in Nome. Having made their fortune as prolific gold miners in the panhandle town, they'd expanded their business and influence into other spheres. Even the hotel Ella had booked online had been one of three not currently owned by a Porter subsidiary.

Avoiding Porter planes, Porter boats, Porter hotels... It was all just going to grow more difficult the closer she got to the town.

The boat captain was still prattling away as he moved up the channel cleared of debris towards the only working docks, used mostly for emergency vehicles and the few coast guard boats kept in repair during the winter.

But even here, ice floated along and they moved slowly towards the docks.

"Huh, looks like you have a greeting party, there, missy," said the captain, nodding towards the wharf.

She had spotted it too. She kept her tone even, clinically polite, completely devoid of emotion. Ella couldn't remember the last time she'd lost her temper. Not even when her boss had confronted her about the debacle on her last case with the Virginia field office. Not even when he'd said she was being reassigned to nowhere.

Not even when she found out *nowhere* meant her own hometown. As the lost princess of the Porter empire, it felt like returning home with her tail tucked between her legs. But ever the dutiful soldier, ever obedient and ever accommodating, even in defeat, she'd taken the assignment. Then again... it wasn't *fully* out of magnanimity, was it? No... No she hadn't wanted them to look too closely. At what had happened with the arrest. The escape. And her involvement in it.

A pang of guilt and fear jolted through her, but she swallowed, keeping her expression stony.

As for her career, what else could she do? Hopefully, after a year of penance on these snowy shores, they'd let her return to the lower-forty-eight. Anywhere, would do. Anywhere except home.

But now, the homecoming party was out in full array.

Two police vehicles sat on the wharf, lights flashing, figures in dark coats leaning against the hoods of the vehicles, watching as her transport boat pulled slowly into harbor.

She shivered, wrapping her hands around her arms and blowing air which turned to mist as it plumed past her face and over her shoulder. Her upturned, celestial nose had turned red in the cold. Her eyes were the color of the Bering Sea, a pale sort of blue. Her hair was like the source of her family's fortune. Pure blonde, a golden hue that caught the sun streaming through the sea-spray speckled windshield.

She gripped a metal rail to her side as the boat rocked a bit, the captain guiding them to avoid another chunk of ice.

The mountains in the distance, the fresh, crisp air, the carpet of ice and snow draped over everything as far as the eye could see... it conjured feelings in her chest that she didn't quite know what to do with. The captain gave her another sidelong glance, watching her out of the corner of his eye as he pulled slowly to the dock closest to where the two police vehicles were waiting.

"What did you say your name was again?" He asked. "Eleanor?"

She didn't even grimace at the familiar name. Only her parents called her Eleanor.

"Not... Porter, is it?" the captain said suddenly, his eyebrows rising.

"I don't believe I ever mentioned my last name," she said with a sweet smile and quick nod. She rested her hand on his shoulder in an affectionate pat, and then she turned, grabbed her brown, leather bag, hefted it and moved towards the gray, steel door which led out onto the deck so she could access the wharf.

"Need'm to carry't for ya?" the captain said, his accent thicker as he nodded towards her bag.

She paused, and then gave a brief shake of her head. He had taken another sip from his bottle when she'd turned. But his lips were moist. The *clink* of the glass against metal. The shift of his bulk, and the uncomfortable way he was leaning to the right, disguising any movement of his hand...

"No, thank you," she said politely. "I'm very grateful for all you've done." She didn't say anything about the drink. Ella's attention to detail, and her memory were two of the biggest factors in her success... Not the *biggest* factor. No. The *main* reason she'd succeeded as an agent had to do with a part of her most never saw.

She didn't let them. And with good reason.

Some of her colleagues were tough as nails and wanted people to know it. Others were cold and calculating. Ella, though, strongly believed that one could catch more flies with honey and a will of iron. She couldn't remember the last time she'd lost her temper—not because she didn't feel anger just like everyone else. But because she released it in *other...* more... *interesting* ways.

But more than that... She'd grown up in a family legacy that saw the "little people" as little more than pawns to be used, tools to be discarded when finished with.

She'd spent most of her life refusing to give in to such sentiments. Hours speaking to the relatives of victims, even well past the point of gathering information on a case. Interrogating subjects in prison but often offering food, water, phone calls. Even visiting killers she'd caught to speak with them, showing a bit of human compassion.

It was exhausting.

For the four years she'd spent working at the FBI, she'd lived a life of deference, of protocol, attempting to bring some form of warmth to an otherwise cold workplace.

But now... heading into the heart of a storm-bound city, the warmth was fading. The cold had returned, and it took everything in her to keep that smile affixed as—bag in hand—she hopped off the boat and onto the moldered, wooden dock, the air smelling of both salt and fish.

She gave a nod towards the police officers waiting on the dock, careful-ly stepping over the gap between the boat—the rubber guards—and the dock. Steadying herself by gripping a mooring post, she then straightened, stomping her feet on the dock to return some of the feeling to her toes, then turning towards the figures by the cars.

Two figures were walking towards her—but though they'd come in police vehicles, they weren't cops. She hesitated in confusion, studying the approaching duo. One of them, short and stocky, wearing a black cap. The other, though, a blonde woman, with an upturned nose and light blue eyes. She was pretty like a cheerleader, emphasizing her appearance with a tasteful amount of makeup, a few curled bangs allowed to bob free and seashell earrings.

The approaching woman was the spitting image of Ella.

And as she drew near, Ella went still, the tightness in her stomach only ratcheting up a few notches. She shot a quick glance back towards where the boat captain was excitedly tapping against the window, pointing at Ella and then at the other, identical woman. "I knew it was you!" he exclaimed, his voice muffled by the glass but released by the open window near his elbow. "Eleanor Porter! Welcome back!"

She kept her face a mask. Another mannerly nod. And then she turned to face the twin sister she hadn't spoken to in nearly ten years.

"Ella," said Priscilla Porter.

"Cilla," Ella replied, her voice losing some of its warmth. Her smile remained affixed, but she knew it wasn't reaching her eyes.

"You're late," said the pretty blonde woman, arms crossed now, one foot angled towards Ella. The stocky man at her side had tan skin and was missing a tooth under his upper lip. He scowled at Ella, watching her with a mask of distrust. She didn't recognize the man, but didn't comment on the openly hostile glare. Again, focusing on details. The man stood a bit too close to Cilla. Not an affectionate stance, a protective one. She cataloged this information for later use.

"I wasn't expecting a welcome party," Ella said, her attention back on her sister.

A silence hung between them briefly. Ten years of no letters, no emails, no calls. Ten years of no interaction. And yet things hadn't changed much: the same unspoken hostility emanating from Priscilla and Ella's same dogged determination to ignore the inarticulate things between them.

At last, though, her twin sister shrugged, her jacket sleeves crinkling. "You're a couple hours late. We were expecting the new fed this morning."

"Apologies. We had some engine trouble."

Cilla snorted. "*Apologies*," she muttered. "Hear that?" She glanced at the man at her side. The way he stood, scowling, his hands hovering near his waist where a gun easily could have been hidden under his jacket, Ella guessed this mean-mugging member of her welcome party was private security. Most of her family traveled with bodyguards. Ella had always refused when younger, and it had been no small headache for her father.

"Look," said Cilla with a shrug. "We don't need feds. Never needed the last one, either. But you're here, so there's that."

Ella nodded once. "There's that." She was beginning to shiver, the cold getting to her, but she refused to give her sister the satisfaction. She had always been able to keep her emotions in check but could also keep her face inexpressive. The perfect poker player on Thursday nights after hours... At least, she had been—back in Virginia. Another lance of regret shot through her.

She allowed the cold nip of the wind against her cheeks to jar her from the temptation of self-pity. Gripping the handle on her bag, she approached the nearest parked car. "This one mine?" she asked as she brushed between her sister and the bodyguard.

Cilla then said something that caused Ella to stop mid-motion.

"Can't take you to the office just yet. There's a body."

Ella frowned, turning sharply back. "When?"

"This morning. Out past East Wharf, on the ice. A small gold-mining set up."

Ella glanced at the snow, the frozen sea like some icy desert. "People are still mining in the cold?"

Cilla shrugged. "Not my family," she said simply.

My. Not *our.*

"Dredge mining?"

Cilla nodded.

"Someone's dead?"

"That's what finding a body means, doesn't it?" said Cilla with no attempt to conceal her sarcasm. "Thought they taught you lower-forty eight cops to think for yourselves, yeah?" She said it with a little chuckle pretending to be playful but there was a mean flash in her sister's eyes.

Thought they taught you Alaskan princesses not to be complete assholes, Ella thought. But what Ella said was, "I guess. So…" She hefted her bags. "Should I drop these off, or…"

"Your call. GPS in that car has your office and your hotel programmed in already. Also has the police station—we've set you up with a liaison."

"What type of liaison?"

"Oh, you know." And there was a happy note in Cilla's voice that sent shivers down Ella's spine. "Just someone from around here to show you the ropes. It's been a while. Things have changed."

"I don't believe I need a tour guide."

"I gotta insist," said Cilla. "The liaison is also a good way to earn some trust around here. As I'm sure you remember, sister, gold is cheap in Nome. Trust is pricey. Couldn't hurt to be seen around with a local. Especially as you're the only fed we've got now."

Ella sighed, another feather of icy air rising from her lips, but then she pointed towards the nearest car, quirking an eyebrow in question. At a nod from her sister, Ella then opened the front door of the stationary vehicle, slipped inside and shut the door.

She noticed the engine for this car had been turned off, only the lights left going to drain the battery. But inside, the vehicle was even colder than it had been outside.

Her sister's waiting vehicle, on the other hand, was purring, the engine rumbling as Cilla and her bodyguard approached the front seats.

The whole time she'd been speaking with Cilla, Ella hadn't been able to ignore a simple fact. These two cars were police vehicles. And yet Priscilla Porter was *not* law enforcement. Neither, by the looks of things, was the man at her side.

So how did her sister have access to two cop cars?

Ella shook her head, only frowning now that she had a moment alone. The Porter family's reach was expanding, it would seem. Now even the cops were working as a shuttle service for the tycoons.

Ella, though, wanted nothing to do with it. She turned away from the docks, moving back up the street, giving a faint raised hand towards her sister. Cilla did not wave back, and Ella didn't care. She kept to the speed limit, though; these weren't posted in this section of the town. Some locals were notorious for tearing down things like speed-limits, traffic lights, city ordinances. Thinking of Nome as the wild west during the height of a gold rush only *partially* communicated the air of self-governance and suspicion of outsiders.

A single stop sign, near the dock, had been shot up so badly, it looked more like a bad case of acne than a traffic sign.

Granted, most of Nome wasn't nearly as rough around the edges. But the sentiment of a tight-knit community was ever present. She'd heard stories of strangers visiting the area, sometimes building their own dredges, only to be shot at by local toughs for lingering too close to coveted coastline.

She sighed as she drove down the street, following the GPS. Her sister had shown up to greet Ella—not out of any sense of a familial bond but out of a clear declaration.

I'm watching you. I know when you're arriving. I know where you're going. I'm watching.

It had always been the same with her family. They believed, because their roots went deep, all the way back to the Norwegian who'd helped found the town, that they were entitled to the place. People treated the Porter family like royalty.

As a child, Ella had been something of a princess. Certainly a reluctant one. Some people simply weren't cut out for aristocracy. Her family's parties, hosted in their mountain-side mansions were stuff of legend. They even had an honest-to-goodness ballroom under dazzling, salt-rock chandeliers.

But Ella wanted nothing to do with the Porter legacy.

She was here to catch bad guys. And bury old secrets.

Here, in part, to prove she still had what it took. And then, after a time-out, time-served, hopefully, the higher-ups back in Virginia would relent and allow her to return.

Because if not...

She shivered, staring through the windshield at the winter wilderness beyond the town limits...

She wasn't sure if she would make it. Or if the skeletons in her own closet, after what she'd done on that *last* case, would come back to haunt her.

Something buzzed, and she shot a quick glance towards her phone, which she'd set on the cushioned seat at her side. A notification from the local police department. Her liaison, perhaps. A crime scene only twelve miles from here, along the coast, on one of the icy mining platforms.

She breathed slowly, keeping her emotions in check, the mist fogged in front of her. Her hands gripped the steering wheel, and she glimpsed the edge of her arm. Bare, pale skin.

She frowned at her wrist as she passed down the main street, the sidewalks, the buildings, the vehicles all hidden under mounds of snow. She had remembered, at the age of sixteen—having graduated two years early from the local high school—how she had wanted to get a celebratory tattoo. She'd even had her boyfriend, at the time, sketch out a scene of a forest and blinking owl. She had wanted to wrap it around her wrist.

When she'd mentioned the plan to her parents, they'd instantly shut down the idea.

She'd overheard them discussing the issue in their family mansion's enormous kitchen.

"Can't let her, Lois," her father had said to her mother. "I have that new lease coming up—the family photo in the paper is gonna cinch it. Trust me... Maybe after the photo. If she wants to ruin her skin, let her."

"Of course... and with her complexion?" Her mother had replied. "What is that child thinking?"

It was only one in a long line of experiences with her family where she'd realized the reputation of the Porter household, the money to their name was the most important thing. They hadn't wanted her to get a tattoo because they didn't want it to ruin a photo op for the paper.

Eventually, she'd escaped this town.

But in some ways, she often feared that *now* money controlled her life just as much as it had before. Her clothing was used. She never bought anything new. Ever. This was her own little rebellion. Her phone was seven years old. Her laptop, similarly aged. Her technology often was slower than that of colleagues, but it was a matter of quiet defiance. One of the few areas she allowed herself to live in such a way. She didn't own a car. She had always rented cheap. She didn't like eating out, and if she ordered in she always tipped double.

It was ironic, really, what was now bringing her back. She'd allowed the Graveyard Killer to escape custody. A prolific murderer operating in the lower-forty-eight who would leave his victims in graveyards. The killer had murdered seventeen people by the time Ella had caught up with him.

And then...

She'd let him get away.

But Nome was where secrets came to hide, buried under the ice, hidden in the sea.

Perhaps it was the right place for her after all.

She shivered, rubbing her steering wheel, feeling her stomach twist. Her phone beeped with an alert, the cracked screen displaying a notification.

Coordinates. The text said. Sent again by the police liaison, she supposed. She shivered again, double-checked the heat was on, then realized the unit was broken. She scowled, absolutely certain her sister had intentionally given her a car with a broken heating unit in the heart of the frozen town.

With trembling fingers, which she blew on to warm, she texted back. *On my way.*

And then she plugged the coordinates into her own GPS. The small dashboard positioning system was a tempting offer, but she wouldn't put it past her sister to mark the wrong locations just to ruin Ella's first day on the job.

As she sped along the street, following the chirping voice from her phone's outdated GPS, she shot a quick look at the fuel gauge.

Orange. On empty.

She scowled, glancing up the road, searching for the nearest refueling station. She hadn't had a chance to unpack, but the Porter family's welcome carpet was already rolled out in full.

She wasn't here to play games with Priscilla, though. She was here as the sole agent currently assigned to the field office.

And according to her sister, a body had been found.

Unpacking could wait. Finding her hotel could wait. If there was *one* thing in life she'd ever been good at, it was catching killers.

And for most of her career, she hadn't let them go.

CHAPTER 2

THE GLOVES AND HAT and scarf she'd purchased from the gas station smelled faintly of the stale rotisserie hotdogs she'd spotted above the rack. Not technically *used* clothing—a personal policy. But one dollar gloves were as bargain barrel as she could find.

Plus, it was just so damn cold.

She pulled her refueled SUV to the side of the road, hopping the curb in order to clear a path in the snow and shoving open her door with a booted foot. She slammed the door behind her, jamming her gloved hands into her pockets and marching through the snow towards where a man was waiting for her, sitting on a snowmobile.

The *liaison,* she supposed, was watching her. His face was hidden behind a ski mask. He held up a thumb.

She returned the gesture.

"You're the new fed?" the man called out. His voice sounded somewhat familiar, but she was too distracted to place it. He also wasn't looking directly at her, busy with his machine, adjusting the mirrors, checking the fuel.

She nodded. "Just the snowmobile?"

"Yeah,," he said with a shrug. His voice was tight, unfriendly. *Cold* was perhaps the right word. Not a warm voice. Not at all. An icy, frigid voice. But still, he gestured for her to get onto the back of the snowmobile.

"Are you the liaison with the Nome police department?"

He shook his head.

"Wait, you're not?"

Another shake of his head. "I'm marshal's service," he said simply. "But I am your liaison."

"Hang on... I thought you were supposed to be police."

He shrugged. "Sorry to disappoint," he said, still fiddling with his mirrors. "You coming?"

She frowned now. "Do you know where they found the body?"

He nodded once. "I found it."

"Oh, alright. How far?"

"Minutes or miles?"

"Either."

"Ten minutes. Here, hold on to the back of my sleeves. There. You been on one of these before? Just make sure to grip the—"

She hopped onto the snowmobile, moving slower than she might have in order for her action not to feel like a direct rebuke to the man. She *had* been riding snowmobiles since she was six. But out here, she needed all the allies she could get. To reach the mining camp, built on the ice, they'd have to go the rest of the way on the lighter machine in order to avoid cracking through the ice and plunging into the Bering Sea.

She shivered at the prospect.

She grabbed the seat, held onto the metal handles under the front seat, instead of his sleeves, then gave a cheerful nod.

He spotted the motion in one of his mirrors, then called over his shoulder, "Tap me twice if we gotta slow. Otherwise, we're going quick."

He had a thick jacket on, along with snow goggles and an upraised hood, making it difficult for her to discern much about him. But he certainly reminded her of something—it was in his voice. There was a heavy, somber way in which he spoke, as if each uttered word cost something of his will.

She shivered now, held on, and away they went, skidding over the snow towards the crime scene. She couldn't remember the last time she'd taken a *snowmobile* to a murder scene.

In every direction she looked, she spotted more flat ice—a blanket of white wherever she glanced.

Even as she gripped the handles jutting from beneath the black, cushioned seat, they picked up speed. The snowmobile itself was unfamiliar to her. The front half didn't match the back, as if someone had combined two different vehicles, likely stripping one for parts to outfit the other. An impressive display of mechanical know-how, if nothing else.

Similarly impressive was her current liaison's snowmobiling skills. He avoided clumped ice and rivets with gentle tugs or redirects of the handlebars. Not once did they slow, nor did he seem to lose his nerve.

Ella smiled as they picked up speed. As much as she hated the ocean—things like *this?* She could remember para-gliding in Panama. Could remember spelunking with one of her old partners after collaring a serial killer. Could remember fast laps around the race-track in more than one supercar. She would never speed illegally—perish the thought. She followed the rules to the letter. But that didn't mean she hadn't already completed a hundred jumps for her skydiving permit. And before she'd been kicked out of her old field office, she'd even been working on her pilot's license.

Her favorite part after a breakneck race over open waters on jet-skis or following a slaloming race down a triple diamond ski slope, was how when she turned up the next day in a business suit, wearing a professional smile, her hair bobbed and looking something like a retired cheerleader, no one at her office knew a thing about it. No one except her partner and the occasional friend.

There was a power in being underestimated.

And so, as she held onto the handles and the snowmobile picked up speed, breaking eighty, easily, ninety, faster… Snow and ice flung on either side as they tore over the terrain and left a billowing cloud behind them, suddenly gave her the view of a small, mining encampment set against the ice.

They rapidly approached the visible spot. A single, orange tent—shaped like a yurt—jutted from the snow. An opening in the ice stood like a dark mark in the white. She glimpsed a small, gray generator, occasionally speckled with snow. The fact that the generator wasn't covered in ice suggested to her that it was either still running or had only recently been shut off.

"When did they find the body?" she yelled into the ear of her driver.

But he didn't even hear and instead, put on a final burst of speed, carrying them easily past a hundred miles per hour before he twisted the handles in a slick move that sent them skidding the final twenty feet towards camp, spraying an arch of sludge against the orange yurt.

Now, she felt certain, he was just trying to show off.

As the engine died, the adrenaline faded, and they came to a full stop, the man was nodding his hooded head in appreciation.

"You're a bit of an adrenaline junkie, huh?" said the man, chuckling now. "I even gunned it there—most yuppies are screaming for me to stop at about sixty." It was the first note of good humor in his voice. Up until this point, his tone had only sounded somber. Now, he dismounted from the snowmobile, finally turning to get a good look at her. And as he did, he tugged at his ski mask, revealing his features.

This done, brushing past wild bangs, he looked at her—no longer fiddling with the machine, nor pointedly looking away from the new-coming stranger to his town.

He froze.

Ella, who was also stepping from the snowmobile, also went still. They stared at one another, stuck in place.

That absolute jerk! Ella thought, thinking of her sister. But instead, she said, "Oh."

The man across from her scratched his prickly chin. "Huh," he replied. He did a double take, as if making sure of something. Likely wondering if he was looking at Priscilla. Most of the folk in Nome knew Cilla had a twin.

And if *anyone* would be able to decide *which* sister was standing across from them, it would be this man.

"Hey, er, Brenner," she said uncomfortably, shifting from one side to the other, and rubbing at her extended arm, ruffling her coat's sleeve with gloved fingertips.

He was frowning though. His handsome features tightened, his blonde brow pressing low over his narrowed eyes.

God dammit, she thought. He'd gotten even prettier with age. Those blue eyes, that chiseled jaw. A single burn mark, though, traced under the side of his chin, up to his left ear. He scratched at it, absentmindedly, studying her with his solemn, blue gaze.

"Well gosh," he said. "Cilla didn't say it was you."

"Well, yeah."

"Been some time."

"I guess so. How are you?"

"Nah, don't do that."

"Oh, okay."

"Shit, don't do that either."

"Do what?" she said, holding back a frown.

He waved a gloved hand at her, waving up and down. "That—don't do *that*!"

She said, "You just waved at all of me."

"You know what I mean, El," he said.

"Don't call me that, Brenner."

He snorted. "We doing that? Fine—call me Mr. Gunn."

She felt her lips tighten into a thin line, but she still didn't frown, as if keeping her eyebrows raised was an exertion of concentrated will. She found her anger slowly receded. Some might say *repressed.* But it was moments on that snowmobile that allowed her to safely excise hidden resentment.

Plus, the job she'd been given, the job she *loved,* had served a similar purpose.

Sky-diving, spelunking, paragliding—all fun, all exciting. But it paled in comparison to collaring a murderer. To hunting a serial killer and facing down with them in some dark hotel, or late at night while stalking his next victim.

That was the ultimate adrenaline rush.

She glanced towards the snowy ground, frowning. She spotted a figure laying in the snow next to the ice.

"Where's the coroner?" she said quietly.

"Rushing back from an elk hunt," Brenner Gunn replied.

She shot him a look.

He pointed at her face. "See, *that.* Poker face Ella. You still doing that, hmm?"

And are you still drinking? She wanted to bark back. Instead, she said quietly, "I don't mean to offend you, Brenner."

"You took care of that twelve years ago," he shot back, adjusting his gloves now, and turning to stomp towards the body she'd spotted.

Now that his back was turned, she frowned briefly and skipped through the ice to catch up. "Hang on one moment," she protested. "That's not fair. You're the one who broke up with *me* remember?"

He paused now, near the open hole carved into the ice. His handsome features were tinged with red from the cold. As he adjusted his gloves, she spotted markings along his wrist. Tattoos. He hadn't had those when they'd been dating. He'd probably sketched the designs too—the same way he'd done when she'd wanted one but gotten cold feet. She'd always envied Brenner's drawing skills.

Brenner Gunn and Ella Porter. The two of them had started seeing each other in middle school. They'd lasted five years, which—as far as young love went—wasn't a bad stretch.

At one point, Ella had even thought she would marry Brenner, though, she hadn't voiced this *too* loudly to anyone. She could remember the feeling when he'd broken up with her. After five years of dating, he'd called it quits.

Had never even told her why.

Brenner Gunn had been another name she hadn't wanted to hear ever again. This reassignment was starting to feel more punitive than she'd first thought.

"You staring at my ink?" he said, his voice cold again. The humor she'd heard earlier was gone. The way he chose his words and uttered them, seemed as if each effort in speech was both mentally and emotionally taxing. "I remember," he said. "Too good to date a guy with tattoos, right?"

She hesitated, studying the man. He was a few inches over six foot. The way he was speaking, though, the belligerent tone—she remembered that as well. Good-looking didn't always mean good character.

In fact, it often didn't.

"Are you drunk?" she said quietly, her tone gentle, attempting not to be accusatory.

And now that she studied him closer, she noticed the red rings around his eyes, the faint sway in his step as he approached the hole in the ice. She also felt a little shiver of fear. The man had been flying over the ice at the speed of a Ferrari, and by the looks of things, he wasn't sober.

She let out a little huff of air, feeling even more animosity rising in her chest. She didn't blame Brenner. He hadn't asked for this assignment. She blamed Priscilla, and—undoubtedly—her parents.

The chance to assign her to pair with her high school ex-boyfriend had clearly been too sweet an opportunity for them to pass up.

He didn't reply to her question. Instead, his voice somewhat bitter, he muttered, "Coroner should be here with forensics in an hour or two."

"You are drunk."

"I mean, the stiff *is* frozen. I found it four hours ago anyhow."

"Brenner," she said with a sigh, "I can't do this right now. I can't keep pretending there's no history in this godforsaken place. Did you *ask* to partner with me on this?"

He shot her a stunned look, his blue eyes widening, still ringed red. "You think I'd ask?" he snorted. "God dammit, Ella." He blinked a few times and swayed. "You're as gorgeous as ever, you know that?" he let out a little hiccup, and then stumbled back, reaching out swiftly and catching himself against the snowmobile as if he didn't need it to stay upright.

Ella was given another glance at his arm tattoo. She blinked in surprise. "You really did it?"

"Hmm?"

She had gone still by the icy opening in the sea, near the body, but briefly, her eyes were captivated by the trident tattoo. "You really did join up, then? The Navy?"

He shrugged. "Couple of years."

"Then the SEALs?"

He nodded. And for a brief moment, the sad, somber look in his eyes faded. He smiled and murmured, "Happiest five years of my life."

For some reason, this comment stung. "So you're a U.S. marshal now?"

He chuckled bitterly. "Not fit to blow shit up, they say." He tapped his hand against his knee. "Too much damage to the knee, I guess. Let's just say I only go fast on machines now."

She paused, exhaling again.

At a normal crime scene, there would have been droves of people. Police, coroner, forensics, tech, beat cops standing sentry. News crews trying to peek.

But out here... another body? Little more deserving than a rumor traded over a cold beer in a semi-warm bar after a day of labor. Work in a place like Nome was the type of work done with hands. With bent backs. Mechanics, crab-fisherman, gold miners, diggers, dockworkers.

This wasn't a place for the gentle-hearted.

Once upon a time, she'd thought Brenner was just that. A gentle heart. But she didn't recognize the man sitting in the snow. Not anymore.

The ex-Navy SEAL pushed to his feet, wobbling a bit on his injured leg, and then he turned to face the body. Neither of them said anything for a few moments.

The tension wasn't just awkward. It was also sad.

Ella didn't know what to think, nor did she know what to say. And after his brief emotional outburst, Brenner's tone went cold again. "Stabbed," he said simply, pointing towards the injuries in the man's back.

"No blood," she said, pointing in the snow.

"He wasn't in the snow."

"Right—in the water, yeah? His jacket is frozen stiff."

Brenner snorted, shooting her a look. "So FBI, huh? That's where you ended up. For real—you're an honest to goodness fed? Ever collar anyone?"

She smiled. In a way, it felt like a high school reunion where she was the only one who hadn't added any extra poundage.

Then again... if anyone in town knew the true story about her exile? She shivered, closing her eyes. "Yeah, I guess so," she murmured. "Some."

"Beautiful and smart then..." He nodded, sad.

For a moment, she frowned when he wasn't looking. Twice now he'd complimented her appearance. The last thing she needed out in this icy wasteland was for an old flame to try and come back and warm her.

But as she studied him a moment longer, she realized he wasn't coming on to her.

Rather, he was occasionally glancing at her like a spectator peering at an animal in the zoo, behind thick glass. A divide between them. No way through, though the barrier seemed transparent.

His voice was somber. His eyes deeply, deeply mournful. She felt her heart twinge at the sight of her ex. Inwardly, she swore to double-check *any* assignment Cilla had a hand in. And then, feeling the weight of grief settling on her, as if transferred by the tone in Brenner's voice, she dropped to her haunches, studying the body in the ice. Glancing at the water then up again.

"Anyone in the tent?"

"None."

"Do we know who this is?"

"Yeah—Baron Jones."

"Did Mr. Jones lease the Revcot himself?" she said, looking up, surprised. Her eyes scanned the cold terrain. "Thousand acres on the Rev, right?"

"Something like. Nah, Jones was just a sidekick. He worked for Longstreet."

Ella wrinkled her nose. "My dad's old secretary?"

"Not anymore. Longstreet hit it big on some inland pay five winters ago. He's now big britches around here. At least, for dredge mining."

She whistled, her lips cold. She looked back at the dead man. No blood in the snow. Then she said, quietly, "Who was his diver?"

Brenner just frowned at her.

She pointed at the generator. "Air line there. Hot water line there. Sluice box still has pay dirt in the catch. There was a diver. He's not suited up. No second, you said."

Brenner stared, and then his eyes widened. "Shit, you're saying—"

"We might have a second body," she replied softly. She winced, glancing around in the snow, pausing to duck into the orange tent. But the inevitable conclusion stared her in the face. The air line and hot water line were still in the hole. The body had been *found* in the hole.

Brenner followed her gaze until both of them were staring into the Bering Sea. "You don't think he's still down there, do you?" he whispered.

She shrugged. "You're a SEAL, right? You have a suit?"

"No. But I can get one in five minutes. Uncle lives on the coast that way, but he'll be ice-fishing."

"You're sure?"

"He's always ice-fishing. I can grab a suit. You coming with or staying here?"

She glanced at the snowmobile. Suddenly, the seat looked far too small, and the vehicle would be far too crowded for the both of them.

"I'll hang back," she murmured. "Hurry."

"What's the point? Air line is dead. If anyone's down there, so are they..." Still, Brenner complied, hopping back onto the snowmobile, gunning it and kicking up crystals as he sped away.

She stared after him, shivering in the snowy terrain and frowning as he left.

Of course, he was right. If anyone was still down there, this would quickly turn into a double-homicide.

And only her first day back in town.

CHAPTER 3

She felt weightless, hovering in the water, kicking to keep herself aloft. Her head poked from the water, through the burrow hole, and she tried not to think of the body floating in the frigid cold, exactly where her head currently protruded. The goggles were a bit too large for her face, but the suit fit snugly.

This, in part, was the reason *she* was going under instead of Brenner. The suit his uncle had provided was simply too small.

She wondered, vaguely, if Brenner had done this on purpose. But she'd kept most of her clothing on when changing into the diving suit, even entering the orange yurt for privacy.

There was only one small flaw in the plan.

"What do you mean it's cut through?" she said, frowning over a useless mouthpiece.

The US marshal frowned down at her, shrugging his broad shoulders. "I mean completely severed," he said. "Someone snipped the airline. We can call for tanks, but it'll take some time."

"And the coroner is still an hour out?"

"At least."

She frowned, shaking her head in frustration, bobbing in the freezing water. It was warmer, however, now that the hot water was cycling through her suit. She could feel the way portions of the rubber inflated, like the veins inside some blubbery animal, allowing the warmth to spread through her body and encase her form in a thin, insulating layer of warmth to help trap her own body heat.

Hypothermia was secondary to the threat of drowning under the ice.

She sighed slowly, causing a faint ripple in the water under her chin. She adjusted the chin guard of the scuba suit, making sure as much of her skin was protected from the frigid depths.

"No waiting," she said finally. "Just keep an eye on me, alright?"

Brenner just watched her, his gaze unflinching.

She then shrugged, flashed a thumbs up, and began to inhale rapidly. She flooded her system with oxygen, hyperventilating. And then she adjusted her goggles, turned and dove into the water without a second glance back.

And again, the same way it had felt speeding on the snowmobile, she felt a surge of excitement as she ducked into the dark, frozen sea, under a roof of ice. The murky water swept up towards her.

Her fear of the ocean, of the dark water, only made her more alert. She felt her stomach twisting in anxiety. A familiar sensation.

But in the same way she'd once been scared of heights and now had a sky-diving permit, the small, cherubic FBI agent, who most people thought was too accommodating, too painfully polite to be much of a threat, dove into the very source of her fear.

Her skin prickled, a few jolts of cold along her cheeks where the mask didn't quite meet the edges of the suit. She kicked—no flippers, she'd refused these—and descended lower into the dark. As she did, she rolled on her back, gliding through the water, keeping an eye on the surface.

No rapid motions. She held her breath, conserving her energy. As she floated slowly to the sea bed, her eyes adjusted in the dark. She spotted a faint glow of light coming from the nozzle of a long hose. A ten-inch by the look of it. Heavy-duty equipment.

Her family didn't get out of bed for anything besides actual back-hoe dredge work or inland sluicing. The vacuum dredges, as her father had called them somewhat mockingly, could get eight ounces a day if manned by an experienced diver. Eight ounces of gold, depending on the market, and depending on the cleanup—especially after removing black sand—could fetch anywhere from sixteen to twenty thousand dollars.

Just for the one day.

In this business, if someone made a killing, it often meant it was the sort of score worth killing for.

And now, illuminated by the faint, penlight glow from the nozzle of the underwater dredge hose, she spotted glinting particles in the sediment. She swam a bit lower.

Gold.

Everywhere she looked, pieces of gold. She even spotted a nugget, the size of her fingernail. Gold on the sea floor wasn't nearly as impressive as some ten-ounce nugget found in a mineshaft. But the old-timers—the name given to the gold-rush prospectors who'd already stripped the mountains—had already taken most of the chunks and nuggets from inland. The real score now lay with the gold *dust* left behind.

Sometimes, inland, in river beds or in deeper pay layers than the old-timers could have dug with their old-fashioned equipment. Ella knew of a couple miners who'd dug more than sixty feet through sheer mud to find a pay layer. The fuel costs alone had taken as much as ten thousand dollars a day.

But the return pay? Even greater.

The gold in the ocean, though, was a bit different. It didn't come from old mines, left behind by the old-timers. Rather, it came mostly from melting glaciers. The currents would bring the gold along the sea floor and wedge it against the coast-line, seeing as the gold was heavier than most sediment.

The glaciers deposited the gold. And the miners swept it up again. Someone had been doing a good job of sweeping by the look of things.

Ella frowned, glancing along the ground, watching the way the diver had expertly scooped up every last crumb in the gravel layer. No gold for ten feet behind her. Everything taken.

And then...

She turned back, shifting a bit, holding her breath as her lungs began to protest. A couple of bubbles burst past her lips. She wore the mouth guard if only to protect her mouth from the cold. But no air—she'd have to keep at least thirty seconds of air to reach the surface.

A minute under so far? She didn't have much longer until her lungs began to ache. Her stomach formed a tight knot, but she knew this was simply fear... And fear was something she'd decided to ignore a long time ago. Fear was the whisper of *don't, can't, careful.*

Her response for years had been. Will. Shall. Won't be.

Her eyes traced the dark gloom, moving over the ground. She hesitated after a moment, biting her lip and tasting salt from where she'd accidentally splashed water into her mouth while above. She glanced up, spotting a shadow over the ice where Brenner Gunn moved back and forth near the opening in the ice.

There was a nervous energy to his limping gait.

That's not right, she thought all of a sudden, staring at the sediment.

She glanced back, making sure she hadn't missed something.

Someone had moved the hose. *After* it had been turned off. A miner wouldn't do that—a diver accustomed to scooping pay certainly wouldn't. It was like leaving breadcrumbs on the floor unswept. Very expensive breadcrumbs.

She glanced through the gloom, redirecting the nozzle's LED lights, illuminating a darker portion of the ocean floor.

More sediment. More streaks in the pay.

The nozzle had been twenty feet to the left and then moved here. Scooped along the ground a bit and then abandoned. That didn't make sense—the section twenty feet to the left had been swept up enough to suggest pay. So why would the diver have moved onto worse ground?

Unless the diver *hadn't* moved the nozzle.

What did that mean?

Someone else had?

Why would someone else move the nozzle, though?

That answer seemed obvious enough. Someone dead above. A diver missing. Gold involved.

Something was being hidden. And by the look of things, whatever that *something was,* occupied the space twenty feet to the left. Someone had even gone to great lengths to leave a field of gold to draw the eye. Whoever this killer was, they weren't a thief.

The diver, perhaps?

Maybe the diver had turned on their assistant. Killing Baron then running for it. Why? Had they found a special pay streak?

Now, her lungs were protesting, but her own curiosity was more potent than the anxiety of drowning. She could feel the fear in her gut. Could feel it physically attempting to crawl up her spine, to tiptoe along her arms with frigid footsteps.

But the fear was compartmentalized now. She thought of her sister's harsh words, and her held tongue. Of Brenner's drinking, and again she'd said nothing. The small wounds, those festering things didn't *go* away. They stayed hidden until released... And it was in acts of will she released them.

She wouldn't rise from the water. Not yet. It didn't *hurt* enough for her to rise.

Her curiosity, the surge of adrenaline as she decided to stay underwater longer than was wise, propelled her through the murk. Now, she plucked one of the hooked lights from the end of the nozzle, fiddling a bit to unclasp it from the ridged edge. She then shone the thing in front of her, allowing the light along the bottom of the sea floor to lead the way.

Sand and sediment gave way to tangled clumps of green vegetation.

And then... she hovered over a second pay streak.

More gold. Even thicker than the earlier location.

And something else.

She frowned. Bubbles now sneaking past her cheeks. Her lungs protested. Another minute and she'd go unconscious. The pain in her lungs, though, was second to the fear. Panic. Anxiety. All flavors of the same.

Sweet. Cherubic. *Nice.* Polite. The names she'd been given. The labels she'd accepted. At first, she'd resented the assumption. Small, blonde and pretty didn't mean she was someone whose cheek needed pinching while being led around by the apron strings.

But she'd then grown to appreciate the mask. Some of it authentic but some of it constructed. A protective disguise, similar to the somber frown Brenner wore.

Another little niggling thought occurred to her.

As she hovered in the water, gripping the hose, staring at the ground, she thought of the SEALs. Brenner had been special forces. Had come home. Had the look of death and pain in his eyes now. Smelled of whiskey. But it was rumored that SEALs were mentally tough enough to stay *under* the water until they went unconscious. They would train, it was sometimes said, until they drowned themselves. And then were brought back and revived.

She didn't know if it was true.

But it was a compelling thought.

To have *that* level of will? Another niggle of fear jolted through her. Of repressed anger.

And so she stayed down longer.

Now her lungs *really* ached. She even found herself smiling behind her mask. She returned her attention to the strange sediment. She reached out, brushing a hand through the gravel layer. Someone had hastily buried something. That much was clear.

But whoever had done it didn't know much about dredge-mining or had been in a hurry. They'd disturbed the sediment and then placed black rock on top of silt. Not the other way around.

Her hand scraped through the sea floor. Trailing through the silt. Strands and ribbons of mud flitted away on the current, carried like smoke on the wind.

And then her fingers bumped something hidden there.

She paused, frowned. Scraped more and tugged.

The bones of an arm came away in her hand. She yelped, dropping the thing, watching where the severed, skeletal arm tumbled to the sea floor. She stared at the fleshless thing. Now there were no more bubbles left *to* exhale. But something had snagged on the skeletal bone. She spotted it—a piece of black rubber—the glove of a diving suit?

Her head was pounding. The pain in her lungs had slowly passed, leaving only an ache, and a deep sense of numbness.

Black spots danced across her vision. But the anxiety... the anger was gone. Thoughts of Cilla's mocking, Brenner's accusations, even the boat captain's questions—they drifted away like bubbles. She still saw the memories, she rarely forgot the details of a recollection, but the negative emotion had bled out, now.

She caught a rock with one hand, placing it on the arm bone to prevent the current from sweeping it away. And then finally, with some air of reluctance, she turned and kicked once, twice. Her motions were cautious, careful.

Where was the hole in the ice?

She winced. Now the dark spots had nearly completely covered her vision.

Now she...

There!

She kicked a couple more times, heading straight towards the opening. And as she shot forward, she felt her consciousness begin to slip.

CHAPTER 4

TOO DAMN LONG.

She'd been down there too damn long.

Brenner Gunn paced back and forth, half limping as he did. He felt his muscles straining beneath his jacket, poised for action. He had half a mind to throw himself in that hole after her and go drag the little pixie from the frost.

Of course, he knew better than anyone that Ella Porter wasn't what she seemed.

Not by half.

Mentally tough. That was mostly how he thought of her. At least, towards the end of their relationship that was how he'd thought.

She had an unbreakable will. Once upon a time, he'd thought of himself as the most stubborn SOB to ever disgrace Nome's shores.

And then he'd met that cute blonde in eighth grade. The two of them had passed notes to each other for a couple of months. Started dating after that.

He'd thought of her as nice. As friendly. As pretty. It wasn't until some years passed that he realized what she really was.

Iron willed. Stubborn as hell.

Stubborn with a smile.

And now she was still underwater. Two minutes passed. He double-checked his stopwatch. No. Shit. Nearly three.

He cursed, preparing to rip off his jacket and toss it to the side. He'd have to risk the cold. He knew he shouldn't have let her go down there without air. What had he been thinking?

But no. Not thinking. Damn well drinking, right? Whiskey.

Shit. She'd seen him tipsy. She'd even asked about it. That was why they'd broken up, wasn't it? His drinking. No... no, that wasn't right, was it?

It was so hard to remember. But at least *that* he did remember. He knew why it had ended. And he'd never told her.

He cursed, stomping to the edge of the hole in the ice, flinging his coat to the side. He ripped his sweater off, tossing it as well. The freezing cold assaulted his thin t-shirt. He began to peel this back as well. The sooner he dove in the better. Hopefully, he wouldn't lose any fingers.

Just then, as he prepared to dive, her head emerged.

For a brief moment, staring, he thought her eyes were fluttering. Thought she was unconscious. But then, a deep breath. Some spitting as salt water trickled past her lips, and then with shaky motions, Ella pulled herself from the water. She glanced at Brenner, standing shirtless.

"Nice abs," she said, then she chuckled.

And though she was smiling, teasing, he sensed something shaky in her voice. Fear? Something like it. She was blinking now, inhaling slowly and massaging her forehead as she tugged down her mask and spat more seawater.

"What happened?" he snapped, still trembling and pulling his shirt back on.

She pointed at him. "Same to you."

"I thought I had to dive in for you. God dammit. You were down there three minutes."

She blinked. "Oh—sorry. I didn't mean to upset you, Mr. Gunn."

Mr. Gunn.

The words cut deep. He doubted she'd meant them too. Why in the hell had he chosen to drink today? What a scumbag he was... If he'd known Ella Porter was coming back to Nome, he might have gotten a damn haircut or something. At least he wouldn't have been wasted to meet her on the ice.

Now she saw him as an asshole. A drunk asshole.

She was still blinking, massaging her forehead. She inhaled in and out a couple more times. Then she looked up, wincing as if from a sudden pang. "We need more bodybags."

"What?"

"There's a skeleton down there. A burial site. The site went on a bit, though. Might be more than one body. I also think I saw fragments from a ripped suit. Might be another victim out there, fresher."

"The diver down there?"

"No. These bones were picked clean. Do we know who the diver is yet?" she said, dripping water and struggling to her feet now, leaving the suit on for the moment and allowing the warm water to heat her.

She really was a frail thing. No taller than five foot two. Perhaps a hundred pounds, if that. Pretty as ever. Her celestial nose tinged red. Her piercing eyes, never malicious. Her golden hair, the only thing that seemed to belong in this town.

But Ella Porter was one thing he refused to be.

A liar.

Everything about her, every smile, nod. Every polite comment. Every attempt to placate even the most violent tempers. It was all make-believe. All some large pretense.

She never let people see who she was. She would *never* drink in public. Never do anything to compromise her reputation. He felt familiar bitter tugs at his heart as he reached into his coat, having secured it back in place, his body still trembling violently. He ripped a small metal flask from inside his jacket pocket, tipped it and took a long pull.

The warmth spread down his throat, into his chest.

He looked her dead in the eye as he tipped the flask back again, taking another, longer sip. He even finished with a loud, "Ahhh." A satisfied, satiated sound.

Though he was neither of these things.

As his ex-girlfriend stared at him, memories flitted back. Memories from a decade ago. Memories that still ate at him. Regrets, mostly.

And they all had to do with Ella Porter.

He'd thought life had kicked him in the teeth up to this point. But now, he realized, penance still wasn't paid. And fate had come along… It had taken everything else. Taken his pride. Taken his home. Taken his… A flash of an image in his mind. Smiling lips, curling hair. A child's laugh.

A lance of pain in his chest, and he took another sip.

Fate had taken it all.

And now it was back for more. It wasn't enough to watch him lose it all. Now he would suffer. Assigned to assist Ella Porter. The one good thing he'd had in his life. Coming from a trailer, with more bruises than bucks thanks to a father's flying fist, there hadn't been much chance for someone like Brenner in a place like this. But Ella hadn't seen any of that.

Her family had. That was for damn sure. They hadn't wanted anything to do with him.

But Ella had stuck by him.

And he'd broken up with her.

But he'd never deserved the warmth of her presence. Had never deserved to have any of that. He was lucky he'd tasted it for a few years back in high school. But this was the rest of his penance. Punishment for who he was.

He would be forced to sit close enough to the only true source of warmth he'd ever known in this damn wasteland. But he'd always remain cold.

Another sip, closing his eyes and allowing the whiskey to do its work.

Self-pity wasn't a particularly becoming trait. But a man had to indulge in whatever remained to him.

Besides, the flask was almost empty.

As the morbid thoughts crossed his mind, he heard a sudden growl of an engine. He frowned, glancing up, bleary-eyed. A truck was speeding towards them.

A heavy-duty, thick-wheeled truck, flying over the ice, skidding every few feet but racing directly at them.

"Brenner!" Ella said sharply, surging to her feet. She shot him a quick look, pretending like she hadn't noticed the flask.

Liar.

"Brenner, who is that?"

He stared at the approaching truck. "Idiot gonna sink himself," Brenner muttered. The truck was too big to be on the ice. Already, he could feel the frosty floor shaking. At any moment, he expected the truck to fall through the—

Crack! Splash!

The crack was the back wheels skipping too high over an embankment then hitting the ground, smashing through the ice. The splash was the wheels dipping into the Bering Sea. A whining sound, smoke and spitting crystals, as the truck tried in futility to pull back onto the ice.

And then, fifty feet away, the thick, black truck, still spewing smoke and churning helplessly in the sea, began to slip, skidding back into the water through the cracked ice.

CHAPTER 5

Ella stared, stunned.

Brenner burst forward without hesitation. Shouting as he ran, wincing and holding his right leg—the leg he'd said was injured. But it didn't slow him much. The tall man sprinted across the snow, still zipping up the jacket he'd discarded on the ice.

Had he been about to jump into the freezing water to find her?

She felt a flash of guilt. If he'd gotten hypothermia because she'd been reckless, she would have felt awful.

But now, there he went again. Brenner Gunn off to save the day.

Brenner had always been the sort to put himself in harm's way on behalf of another. Training he'd received back in his family's trailer. Usually, it was his mother he'd protected. And then, when Brenner had turned fifteen, his mother had succumbed to a second bout of cancer. Whispers around Nome, especially in the single trailer park on the eastern outskirts, had suggested that it had been a mercy for Mrs. Gunn. Her ogre of a husband had been merciless. Things had changed for Brenner after his mother died. It was as if his purpose in life had been snatched away. He'd spent so much time between his father and mother, allowing his old man to pummel him black and blue in order to protect his mom, that when the beatings subsided, he'd ended up turning to drinking.

The first time she'd seen him drunk had been at the age of fifteen.

Three weeks later, he'd broken up with her.

And now there he went again, sprinting across the snow, desperate to fling himself in harm's way as if it was his sole commission in life.

She wasn't able to follow as quickly. The hot water hose attached to the pump by the generator, which attached to her suit. Hastily, watching the sinking truck, breathing rapidly, she pulled off the suit, slipping a couple of times on icy slush.

She snatched her jacket where she'd left it just inside the yurt, and—stumbling forward, pulling on gloves, scarf and jacket, she finally managed to break into a sprint, racing desperately towards the truck. The horn was blaring now. The front door opened as the driver attempted to abandon ship. But it didn't open fully, ricocheting off a thick shelf of ice now that the truck was halfway sunk. The back bed was no longer spinning, the sound of the whining wheels completely muffled by the sea.

Brenner had reached the driver's door now, though. He kicked it closed without hesitation. He then raised his elbow, slamming it through the glass. Shards shattered where his elbow hammered.

Brenner then used his jacket sleeve to clear the shards from the frame. And then snapped his fingers. "Come on! Out the window—now!"

A desperate voice screamed, "My truck!"

"It's gone Longstreet—come on!"

Ella reached the truck now just in time, avoiding the water, to reach out and help pull a man built like a lumberjack through the open window of the truck. Had it been a smaller car, she wasn't sure the big man would have fit.

Now, the truck was nearly fully submerged. The lumberjack was shouting desperately as liquid flooded the cabin of the vehicle, the frozen slush nipping at his legs. He kicked a couple of times, the skin on his belly visible as he stretched out the window, dragged by Ella and Brenner.

The two of them pulled the man onto the ice, out the window. Ella winced as a piece of glass sliced through the thickset man's jacket. Another gouged into the exposed skin at his flank. But despite his yelp of pain, the greater threat was the submerging truck.

"Pull!" Brenner was yelling, red-faced from exertion. "Now! Go—go!"

She complied with the directive, heaving as much as she could. But while Ella had many gifts, upper body strength was *not* one of the ones she might list on a resume.

Still, the combined effort and simply providing something solid for the man in the truck to hold on to allowed the driver to escape his sinking vehicle and scramble, at last, onto shore with a desperate shout.

"God dammit, Longstreet!" snapped Brenner. "What the hell, man?"

But Ella was snapping her fingers. "Excuse me, gentlemen, but the ice!" She pointed out more cracks forming where the truck was now little more than a flood of bubbles escaping to the surface.

Ella and Brenner pulled Longstreet away from the edge of the crater in the ice, retreating back towards the orange yurt.

As they tugged the thickset man in the corduroy shirt, visible past his wool coat, they didn't have to bother much after he let out a strangled cry and began stumbling towards the orange yurt on his own accord. Blood was seeping down the side of his jeans from his hip, where she'd spotted the glass gouge. A flap of his jacket fluttered on the cold breeze where it had been slashed, but he was indifferent to the cold and the pain, stumbling forward now.

The same trajectory he'd used when in the truck. And now he continued as fast he could on foot towards the yurt.

Ella quickly reassessed. Briefly, she'd thought perhaps the man was speeding towards them in his truck to attack them.

Now she realized her mistake.

He was trying to reach the yurt. He was sobbing as he surged forward and now she could make out his desperate shouts. "Janice!" he was yelling. "Janice! No, no, no. Baron! No! BARON!" He stumbled next to the body, shaking the dead man.

Ella called. "Hey—hey, don't touch him!"

Brenner caught up with the big man, tugging him off the victim. "Dammit Vince, you're contaminating the scene, moron!"

Having just saved Vince Longstreet's life, Brenner had no aversions to shoving the big man, hard, sending him toppling into a snow drift. But Longstreet, wild-eyed and desperate, didn't stay down. He stumbled, slipping, back to his feet. Ella glimpsed a wide-eyed desperate expression. A thick, orange beard tinged with snow wagged as Vince shook his head wildly.

She didn't recognize the man, but she knew the name. He'd once worked for her father as an assistant for the inland mining operation. Her father had a strict grooming policy, though. The big beard wouldn't have been allowed at the time.

Her father had always valued appearances as well. She doubted driving a truck into the ice would have been smiled upon either.

And the bawling? Also a no go.

She pressed her lips together in disapproval at the direction of her subconscious. Until enumerating them consciously, it was difficult to remember all the rules her family had insisted upon. Rules to protect the family name. Rules to protect the family business.

In fact, she remembered the conversations she'd had regarding Brenner Gunn on more than one occasion. She hadn't told her family she'd been dating Brenner. When her sister had tattled one day after school, having spied on them behind the bleachers, her mother had reacted in disbelief. A scornful little laugh and then the question, "The trailer park kid? The one with that old drunk for a father?"

That trailer park kid.

Brenner had taken comments like that to heart over the course of his life. For years. Weathering the accusations and snide comments until, eventually, they'd simply worn him down. Sticks and stones broke bones. But words broke souls.

"Brenner, get the hell off me!" Vince was screaming, tottering upright and scraping snow from where it had lodged in the crevices of his jacket. His finger pointed accusingly at him. "Where is she?" he said, his voice a snarl. "Where the hell is she?"

"Vince, calm down," Brenner replied, holding out his hands. Ella paid attention to details, and now she spotted Brenner's knuckles. Somehow, in the chaos, Gunn had lost his glove. And his right hand was visible now, revealing callouses, scars. Rough hands used to rough work.

The marshal kept that hand extended, though it trembled from the cold. "Janice was here?"

"Where is she, Gunn—and what the hell is Priscilla Porter doing here!" he growled, turning to her. He pointed at her. "Did you have something to do with this, bitch? This your dad's doing? I told you—come near my family again, and I'd shoot you dead!" He shouted, marching towards her.

But Ella took a quick step back, hands out in a placating gesture. She hadn't even brought her sidearm with her, having left it back with her things. "I'm not Priscilla, sir," she said quickly. "We only found the one body. Janice—this is your wife?"

Vince stared at her, blinking and trying to make sense of everything. He shot a quick look at Brenner, who had slipped between the two of them now, hands still outstretched, but this time, standing in front of Ella, something had tensed in Brenner's posture.

"Is she dead?" Longstreet said, his voice a moan. "God dammit, Brenner is she dead? Where's Janice?"

"We don't know, Vince. She's not here."

Ella noticed how there was no mention of the skeleton found under the ice. Probably best this detail was left unmentioned. But it was true, she hadn't found the diver. Janice Longstreet... Vince's wife.

Now, though, Longstreet had turned and barreled through the open flap of the orange tent. His shouts were lost briefly as the flap closed behind him and he paused to gather his breath. She heard the sound of broken furniture. The sound of toppling items and scattering papers.

"Janice!" he exclaimed, his voice somewhat muffled but emitted like a moaning wail.

Ella sighed softly. "He can't keep destroying evidence, Brenner," she said impatiently.

This was exactly why the crime scenes she usually worked were covered with agents and cops and forensics. Only people who knew how to handle the place were allowed in. Certainly not the husband of a potential victim.

Husbands of victims were usually at the top of a suspect list. She gave a tight-lipped nod towards the tent door as if inviting Brenner to intercede.

But he just frowned at her. "Hell no," he said.

"Pardon me?"

"I'm not your trained monkey. You want him to stop trashing your crime scene, you tell him. None of that nice girl bullshit—you want a stick? You be the stick."

She stared at Brenner briefly, and he stared right back, refusing to look away.

Why was it always the people closest to you who knew how to push *exactly* the right buttons? Because of course, she knew she'd been doing that. The thin-lipped smile, the understatements. She'd *wanted* Brenner to be the bad guy. To handle the grieving widower a bit more roughly than she might have wanted to. Or even been capable of.

But now there Gunn was, calling her on it. He stepped back, pointing at the tent flap.

She bit her lip and then shrugged, turning and marching towards the open tent flap. "Excuse me, Mr. Longstreet!" she called out. "I really, really must insist. Please, sir, you can't be in—oh. Hello!"

Longstreet stepped from inside the tent now, breathing heavily, red-faced and staring down at her where she'd been approaching the yurt. He glanced from the orange fabric frame, towards Brenner. He whispered, "She's not here..."

Brenner shook his head but had tensed again.

And then Longstreet glanced at Ella, his eyes widening. A sudden red flush crept over his features. In a shaking voice he whispered, "You did this... your family did this, didn't you? Ever since I left—your old man couldn't leave well enough alone. You did this!" he was screaming now, spittle flying, turning cold where it struck her cheek.

She winced, reaching up and wiping with a glove delicately. She wrinkled her nose in disgust. "Please, sir," she began.

But nothing else was added as Longstreet's hand shot out, grabbed her by the neck and lifted her a foot off the ground.

CHAPTER 6

Ella began to choke as Longstreet screamed. "Don't 'please sir' me, Porter!" He looked ready to add more, but that was as far as he was able to make it.

A second later, a blur of color shot past Ella from behind. Longstreet immediately lost his grip as Brenner Gunn slammed shoulder first into the big man's midsection with a sound like wet sand, and he released his grasp.

Ella stumbled, gasping, hand leaping up to massage her neck. At the same time, Brenner knocked Longstreet through the tent flap on the ground. The lumberjack-looking gold miner roared, surging to his feet and throwing a punch.

But now Brenner was no longer talking. One moment he'd been trying to save the man's life, and now his eyes as dead as corpse-flesh, he began picking Longstreet apart, one punch at a time. He moved with merciless efficiency.

Even half-drunk, even favoring his left leg, Brenner's fist shot out, catching Longstreet in a kidney. Then his foot caught Longstreet in the gut.

He didn't go for the man's face but instead went straight for the vital organs. One after the other. Punches below the ribs, to the gut, to the heart. Again and again, picking the larger man apart with one blow after another.

"Okay!" Ella protested. "Brenner, stop! Brenner!"

But he punched Longstreet in the ribs again. And now Vince let out a creaking sound like a rusted hinge. Spittle down his lips, trailing his beard, Vince collapsed to his knees, gasping and wheezing, and staring about as if unsure where he was.

Brenner stood over him, breathing heavily, hands at his side, one still caught in a fist. "You want me to stop, Ella?" he asked, staring at her, his eyes red-ringed.

"Yes, please," she said.

"Please? I don't think you mean it."

He punched Longstreet in the chest again. The big man tried to slap away the blow but missed completely.

Brenner avoided the hand easily and stepped back in, fist raised. "Want me to stop, Ella?"

"I said yes, *please*," she said, her face prickling with heat, staring desperately at Brenner. She made a mental note to *never* leave her gun back with her things again. Not in this town.

But Brenner shook his head. "I don't believe you. Please? That calm tone? Stop lying to me, Ella. Tell me what you want? Hmm?" He raised his fist. Vince Longstreet let out a leaking sound, breathing heavily. He was clutching at his guts now and moaning.

Ella felt a flare of horror. "Stop it!" she said, her voice rising in volume.

Brenner grinned now. Somehow, he was bleeding from his upper lip. Perhaps when he'd headbutted Vince off her. His teeth were streaked with red as he stared at her. He pointed at Vince. "Don't touch her. She's not Priscilla." And then he shook his head, spitting to the side and stumbling away from Longstreet, away from Ella. He limped back towards his snowmobile.

"Where are you going?" she demanded.

He waved at her over his shoulder. "More body-bags," he called. "Coroner still an hour out."

Vince Longstreet was weeping and groaning, clutching at his ribs where he lay on the ground. As she stared at him, she heard a sudden clatter and glanced sharply off to the side. A pair of handcuffs rested on the ground at her feet. Then came the grumble of the snowmobile's engine, and Brenner sped away, leaving her standing over Longstreet's sobbing form.

She winced, massaging at her neck and swallowing to make sure nothing had been permanently damaged. She sighed, stooping to pick up the cuffs. She didn't want to cuff the big man. But she also decided she didn't want to see if he'd try to choke her again.

As she carefully cuffed Longstreet, hands behind his back before gently propping him against the wall of the tent, which indented thanks to his bulk, she gave a frustrated little shake of her head, peering back through the tent flap in the direction of Brenner Gunn.

He wasn't the same person she remembered. A decade... no... *twelve years* would do that she guessed.

One moment, rescuing Longstreet from his sinking car, the next pummeling him into a puddle. One moment, stripping his shirt to risk hypothermia and death to save her, the next screaming at her for... who even knew what.

Stop lying. What the hell had that meant?

She shook her head in frustration, closing her eyes briefly and wishing—more than anything—she hadn't returned to this godforsaken, snowy hellscape.

Already three bodies to deal with. A man in cuffs. A drunk on a snowmobile.

And, by the sound of things, a missing gold miner.

She couldn't imagine a way in which her homecoming could have gone any worse.

CHAPTER 7

SHE STOOD IN FRONT of the heating vent, exhaling in satisfaction as warm air blew across her figure. She'd even unzipped her jacket, standing in the coroner's office. The cold refrigerator compartments occupied the opposite side of the room.

But now, standing next to HD monitors, she was treated to the full blast of the heating unit.

"See this?" Dr. Messer was saying, pointing at the screen with a long finger. "A sharp object in the spine. Both of them were murdered, that's for sure."

Ella stifled a yawn, nodding quickly. "Thank you, doctor," she said. "So we're sure there are two bodies?"

"Yes," the coroner said, turning to face Ella now, her wizened features illuminated by the glow from the screen behind her. The images and the buzzing light served like something of a gruesome halo around the white-haired woman.

Doctor Messer's hair was the same color as a snow drift. Her skin was wrinkled in pleasant ways. Smile lines around the lips and eyes mostly. But she wasn't smiling now. And her nose wrinkled in disapproval when she glanced towards the screen. The bones themselves were currently in one of the refrigeration units.

Dr. Messer had an olive complexion and features that hinted at a more native persuasion than Ella's blonde appearance. The older woman was also shaking her head, tapping one of those same long fingers against her lips. "Not like the old days, all of this," she was saying in disapproval. "Stabbed in the back. You know, back in my day, in Nome, people would settle things face to face."

Ella smiled politely. This was the third *back in my day* comment she'd heard so far. A couple of other comments had included how important it was for a woman *her size* to carry a gun at all times. In addition, Dr. Messer had insisted firmly, more than once, that the reason *neither* of them were married was because there were no good men left.

It had taken a few offhand comments, but Ella decided that by *good men,* Dr. Messer meant someone who'd killed at least once in a bare-knuckle boxing competition and had at minimum two sets of mounted antlers on a hand-built cabin's walls.

She wasn't sure what to make of Messer, but decided as far as Nome went, she was somewhat ordinary.

"So both of them were stabbed—do we know with what?"

The woman shook her head. "Not yet. But possibly the same item used on him." She pointed across the room towards a gurney with a large figure under a sheet.

Ella winced at the sheet. Baron's body. She stifled another yawn. It had taken two more hours for the coroner to show up along with a couple of assistants. It had taken another two hours to get everything back to the office, to take the photos and wait for a preliminary report.

And now, Ella was exhausted. Her eyes were drooping. It was still barely evening, but she'd flown through the night, gotten on the boat in Seattle, then spent most of the earliest portion of the morning on choppy waters with engine trouble.

The day had been a relentless series of challenges, and Ella wanted to find her hotel room. But something now stood out.

She frowned at the body under the tarp. Janice Longstreet was missi ng... but Baron's body had been left behind. What if Janice had killed Baron and fled?

And if not...

A cold shiver moved along her back. Did that mean someone had kidnapped Janice? To ransom her husband? Or something worse?

Ella kept her expression inscrutable and even added a note of energy to her voice, if only to keep the tone amenable. "So if all three were killed by the same person, do we have any idea who that might be? Anything on the weapon used? Anything on the preferred hand?"

"Right hand," Messer said quickly. "I'm afraid that doesn't narrow it down much. But our killer is definitely right-handed."

"So the same person. All three?"

"Maybe. Too early." Messer shook her head. "Baron over there was a good kid, though. I liked him. Once went elk-hunting with me, you know." She smiled.

It was a strange thing to hear such words uttered from a face that made Ella think of kindly grandmothers, not jerky-eating bow hunters.

And yet the framed photos on the back wall displayed exactly this. Dr. Messer standing with more than one team of hunters, grinning happily while holding a compound bow, clad in camo and standing with a thumbs-up next to some poor, hapless creature who'd fallen prey to a well-placed arrow shot.

Ella stared in some amusement and also envy at the photographs on the wall. This was not a woman who cared one lick what Ella thought of her.

"Anything else?" Ella said simply.

"Murder weapon isn't a knife."

"No?"

The coroner shook her head. "The wound is too narrow."

"So what? Like some sort of skewer? Maybe an ice pick?"

A shrug. "Maybe. That's your job to find out."

"So a right-handed killer who attacked from behind, stabbing with something other than a knife. Is that what we have?"

"That's right."

"The two skeletons—male or female?"

"Both male. Both small, too. Like you." Dr. Messer shifted a display screen, a beam of light sweeping towards the corpse.

Ella sidestepped the comment with a demure nod. She said, "Thank you for your time, Dr. Messer." Ella stared at the body under the tarp as something caught her eye, given the shift in lighting. She then took a few steps forward, frowning down at the man's fingers jutting under the cloth. She leaned in, studying the knuckles.

Traces of glitter... Gold. Baron wasn't part of the clean-up crew, just a butt-in-chair. So why did he have gold on his knuckles? A thief? If so... why had the trailings been left in the back of the dredge?

Ella straightened, frowning at the thought.

"Thank you," Ella repeated, turning to leave.

The pale-haired woman smiled at where Ella stood, giving evidence as to the cause of her laugh lines. She quickly snapped her fingers. "One second, one second. Do you like oatmeal raisin or chocolate chip?"

"Do I... oh... Umm..."

Ella didn't have time to carefully turn down the offer before the coroner had skipped happily across the room with the energy of a woman half her age, reached one of the refrigeration compartments where bodies were stored, flung open the metal door, snatched a tupperware and returned. Extending the tupperware towards Ella. "Chocolate chip," she said cheerfully. "Homemade!" she added.

Ella stared in suspicion at the corpse cookies. Instead of refusing, though, she accepted one. "Thank you, doctor. I'll get out of your hair, then."

"No, no, no rush. Feel free to stick around."

Ella said, "I wouldn't want to be a bother."

"No bother at all."

Ella hesitated, trying to extricate again. "I should let you get back to it, then."

"I'm actually almost done. It's no trouble, really. Grab a seat."

Ella just stared, flummoxed. But then she realized Dr. Messer's eyes were twinkling. The coroner chuckled, closing her tupperware and saying, "I'm just teasing. If you have to go, just go. Don't spare my feelings—there's too many people that are too sensitive nowadays. Back in my day..."

But Ella was only half listening as she took the chocolate chip cookie she'd been forced to accept and beat a hasty retreat. When she didn't think the coroner was looking, she paused by the waste disposal can near the door, hesitated, then tossed the cookie out of sight, along the trajectory of an arrow labeled *Toxic Waste. Beware.*

She then called out, "Thank you, doctor!"

And she hurried out of the coroner's office, frowning to herself as she did. Three murder victims, then. Two of them with their bones picked clean.

And by the sound of things, Janice Longstreet had been diving. Now she was missing. APBs had been placed. Local cops and the other few members of Brenner's marshal service were on the lookout. But nothing flagged yet.

Janice Longstreet was nowhere to be found. Baron had gold on his knuckles... Though maybe he'd just been curious topside.

If Janice was on the run, she was likely the killer. But if she wasn't? Then her abductor had already proven he was capable of murder.

Things didn't look good for Mrs. Longstreet, and yet Ella felt her jaw tighten as she hastened down the tiled hall leading away from the coroner's, picking up her pace as she rounded a stairwell and moved back towards the parking lot to see if anything had flagged on the APB.

And then, barring that, to go see if there was anything to find out at the Longstreet residence. Janice was either a culprit or a victim. Vince had attacked her.

Investigating them was the best place to start.

CHAPTER 8

Someone had fixed the heat in her car, and she had a suspicion it was Brenner. Nothing had shown up on the APB, but Ella couldn't sit still—the route from the motel, where she'd dropped off her things, to the marshal's office had taken twenty minutes longer than she'd anticipated.

Now, nearly six hours had passed since the incident with Mr. Longstreet. Alaska only took the occasional suggestion from normal seasonal behavior. Long nights, long days—it all depended on the time of year.

And this was one of those long-night times.

"Damn it," Brenner was muttering. "You think Janice is dead? I knew Janice... Tough lady."

Ella didn't reply, feeling something gnawing at her gut. Tough indeed. But if she'd been missing for almost half the day, her outlook was growing grim.

For the last twenty minutes, they'd traversed up long, flat ground, through icy roads as they headed towards the mountains where the Longstreets lived; Ella and Brenner stared through the windshield, watching the night, seemingly lost in their own thoughts. Both of them nervous. Both of them clearly aware that if Janice *was* still alive, then they were on a clock.

And if not? They still had to find her.

Brenner was now tapping fingers against his right leg, occasionally wincing when he tapped too hard. His eyes were not so bloodshot now.

By the looks of things, he'd even shaved the stubble. She shot him a sidelong glance. He glanced back. They each missed the other by a split second, their eyes not quite meeting.

She glanced over again. He looked quickly away.

They continued hastening along icy roads. But Ella was driving, which meant they normally would have stuck within half a mile per hour of the speed limit, but the fear for Janice Longstreet had inched them to five miles per hour over. As Ella felt a buzz against her leg, she glanced down to where she'd rested her phone. She frowned. An unknown number. The area code wasn't one she was even familiar with. She glanced at the message.

It simply read, *I hear you've returned home.* Nearly an instant later, her phone buzzed again. The cracked screen displayed the message, *This is your friend.*

She wrinkled her nose. Friend? What friend? Someone from Nome?

Brenner cleared his throat. "Umm... They're in the new development. One of the big houses. It's... you know. Porter Enterprises."

Ella sighed. "Of course it is." She stared across the dark, snowbound land. The mountains ahead of them served as something of a shelter, cradling the gold-mining town and protecting it from any northern winds.

"It's kinda beautiful, isn't it?" Brenner murmured.

She was grateful to find he wasn't talking about her this time. "What is?"

"All of it," he said. "It's so... pure. You can see tracks sometimes. But go far enough and there's miles without a single snowflake disturbed." He smiled as he stared through the glass. His eyes briefly lost the sadness they'd carried earlier.

She felt her throat tighten. She looked down at her hands clutching the steering wheel, then up again. They were now going ten miles per hour over. The occasional flurry of ice crystals streaked past the car.

Janice was missing. Either killed or abducted. Baron had gold dust on his fingers—a thief? Did he have an accomplice? "All three victims," she said out loud, determinedly keeping on track, "were killed by the same method. The chances that Janice is still alive are pretty low."

"True. It's not Vince."

Brenner clearly suspected her train of thought. "You're sure? How can you be so certain?"

"It's not him. He loved Janice. Like *really* loved her. He's a bit of an asshole, but he didn't kill his wife."

Ella frowned at Brenner. He looked back and didn't look away. "I swear it," he said simply. "He didn't kill his wife. I promise that." He looked away. "Not that my promise is worth much to you anymore."

She wished she could correct him on this point. But he was right.

She barely knew the man.

Still, he seemed so certain. But even if Vince *wasn't* behind his wife's death—kicking over the crime scene, contaminating evidence as he had—there was still a chance that there was some clue at the Longstreet residence. Some clue that led to the reason Janice was now missing.

"Maybe it's a ransom kidnapping," Brenner said simply. "Everyone in town knows he's rich."

"Vince?"

"Yeah."

"Or maybe," Ella said quietly, "Vince was right, and my father hired someone to do it."

Brenner snorted. "You wish that's true, don't you? Would give you an excuse to lock your dad up for a while, at least."

Ella bristled at the comment but kept her face a mask. "Maybe," she said quietly.

"Dammit, don't do that."

She frowned. "What now?"

"You know what..." he trailed off, inhaled, closed his eyes and looked at her again. The sadness had returned. "Just tell me what you're really thinking, alright? You always used to. Not to anyone else, but you would to me. You told me the truth."

"I haven't lied to you, Brenner."

"Not with your words, no."

"What does that even mean?"

The blonde man shrugged, his blue eyes hazy again. "So you think it might be a ransom?"

She nodded, grateful for the opportunity to return to the topic at hand. "I don't know," she said simply. "I hope not. That might complicate things if I'm honest. Kidnappers usually work in groups."

"Right—hey—there, that road up ahead. The one by the sign. Careful here, sections of the road washed out last week."

Ella followed the directions, turning up a road that hadn't been there before. She frowned as she hastened along the snowy ground. Ahead, she spotted lights at the foot of the nearest mountain. Large, luxurious homes, glowing in the night.

But even the mansions seemed like such very small things at the foot of the mountains.

***

Ella closed her door softly as she turned to face the Longstreet residence. Brenner slammed his door as he followed. "This is it," he said, his breath pluming in front of his lips.

She glanced over her shoulder at the large, gray stone house across the street. "Does anyone live there?" she asked.

"Nah. New constructions this lot. Going to take some time to get anyone with enough bank to move in. Your parents' new place is down that way, though."

Ella frowned, following his pointed finger.

The largest house in the small subdivision settled on top of a hill at the foot of the towering mountain. It overlooked the rest of the luxury homes, settled on a double lot with a warm, orange glow emanating from the windows.

Ella looked away from the house. Her parents had lived in a similarly sized home they'd built closer to the city limits. But it made sense they'd wanted to expand away from the rest of civilization.

She had to hand it to them—the views were gorgeous. Mountains behind her, the deep ocean visible before her in every direction.

She heard a faint *crunching* sound and turned sharply.

Brenner had approached the door and was now wincing, pointing at a smashed panel of glass. "It was like that," he said.

She rolled her eyes. "And I'm the liar," she muttered as she marched up towards him.

"There it is," he chuckled. "The snark. The eye roll. I remember that." He reached in through the smashed glass and opened the door.

"You're good at that," she murmured.

"At what?"

"Breaking windows."

"Lotta practice. They called me Breaching Brenner back in the Navy."

"Really?"

He snorted. "No."

"What was it like? Five years you said?"

He dodged the question, though, stepping into the large home, over glass scattered on the tiled ground, and into the atrium. A twin curving staircase welcomed them as they approached. Brenner moved under the staircase, heading towards a study behind another glass door.

Ella paused, surveying the place.

"We're looking for what exactly?" Brenner called back.

"Motive."

"Vince didn't do this."

"We don't know that."

"I do."

"Any motive, then. Doesn't have to be Vince. Gambling stubs. Threatening letters. Signs of an affair. Sleeping in different bedrooms. You know—any motive."

Brenner looked back at her, lingering in the study, then nodded, entering the office.

It was surreal, watching her ex comb through Longstreet's study. But as she watched him, she felt a strange smile curling her lips. Brenner Gunn was *definitely* a risky choice for a partner. Priscilla had pulled strings, no doubt, to assign him as her liaison.

But in a way... it was nice to have at least one friend back in Nome. At least... sort of a friend. She shook her head, deciding now wasn't the time to think too deeply on such matters. She took the staircase, heading towards the bedrooms.

She reached the top of the stairs and faced three doors. The far end of the hall led to a bathroom, evident by the shower she glimpsed through the open doorway. She ignored this room and instead, pushed through the first door. A painter's studio, amateur but impressive paintings lining the wall. By the looks of things, someone had taken to mixing gold dust with paint to add glister to some of the sunset paintings.

The room smelled of acrylic. Empty canvases were stacked in one corner. Newspaper lay on the ground, crinkling beneath her footsteps. She approached a set of paints and an easel against a desk. She spotted a small vial of gold dust. At least two ounces. More than she made in a week at this new field office. She left the gold where it was, though, and glanced under the table.

There was rolled-up parchment. Also blank.

She regarded the picture on the easel. A small, wooden stool sat in front. She frowned, staring. The painting on the easel was half finished, showing seagulls swooping over an ocean. But half the sea hadn't been painted in yet. Most of the canvas was blue, but parts were blank.

"You were planning on coming back," she murmured to herself. Janice Longstreet was just as much of a suspect as her husband. But this easel suggested the woman had intended to return. Which meant the likelihood of her being involved was lower.

Which also meant the likelihood of her being in danger was much higher.

Ella moved away from the art studio, heading down the hall towards the next door. This was the master bedroom.

One large bed. The blankets on both sides, pillows as well, disheveled. She spotted a woman's clothing in the cupboard. A man's clothing in the dresser. The Longstreets shared a room.

She also spotted evidence in the trashcan that the two of them were still sexually active.

Hardly evidence of an estranged marriage.

She glanced around the room, frowning. If Vince hadn't killed his wife, then he had contaminated the crime scene out of ignorance, not intentionality. But then it meant someone else had to be considered for this.

She frowned. Vince had seemed mighty confident that the Porters had something to do with it. Were her parents possibly involved?

A chilling thought.

She moved over to the other dresser, going through the drawers. Empty. One of them had a Bible like someone might find in a hotel. It didn't look as if it had been used in a while.

She spotted a copy of *The Great Gatsby*. This looked like it had been well used many times.

She moved over to the dresser. She went through the bottom drawers, finding mostly sweaters and long pants. In the top drawer, she found a small, black box. It was locked. She shook it a couple of times and something rattled within.

She frowned, and then smashed the box against the dresser. She winced as she did it, glancing sharply towards the door behind her. At least Brenner hadn't shown up to witness this. After giving him grief over the window, she didn't want to be caught in the same crime.

As she scanned the contents of the small black box, though, she whistled. More tubes of gold. At least twelve ounces total. Life-changing money.

But this was a gold-mining family. It wasn't stunning to find they had gold. So what did it mean?

Probably just savings. People could be suspicious around currency used in the lower forty-eight.

She turned away from the dresser, and stepped back out into the hall, moving to the third and final door. This room was completely empty. A single bookshelf occupied the back wall. But there were no books on it. There were no beds. There was no carpet. The room was bare. She glanced around, frowning. A couple of electrical boxes were exposed, wires jutting out, capped off.

"So why are you empty?" She said, frowning around the room.

She glanced at the ground. A thin layer of dust. The room had been empty for some time now.

She moved towards the bookshelf with no books, glancing along. There was evidence in the dust that there used to be books on the shelf. Maybe even *The Great Gatsby*. But if so, where were the books? And why had they been moved?

She studied the ground, acknowledging the thin layer of dust. The Longstreets had been in no hurry to remodel this room. Maybe they had been expecting a child?

Maybe they simply hadn't had the time.

Ella frowned, making a mental note of the sparse room, the missing carpet, the exposed electrical boxes, and the bookshelf with no books.

And then she heard a faint squeak.

Startled, she turned sharply to face the window.

Not a squeak, she realized. A siren. Frowning, she approached the window, her breath fogging a quarter of the glass as she stared out onto the street.

Six police cars were rushing up the street, through the luxury subdivision. The flashing red and blue lights reflected off windows and the sporadically parked vehicles in some of the driveways.

She hesitated, watching as the cars passed in front of the Longstreet house... but the cars kept on going, hastening towards the largest mansion of them all, perched on a hill, occupying a double lot.

The cars were racing towards her parents' new house.

She stared as the last of the police vehicles thundered in the opposite direction. And as she stared after them, a faint chill crawled along her spine.

A sudden knock sounded on the door behind her. She whirled around.

Brenner was standing there, waving a small, brown, leather book. "Found something," he said.

"So did I," she replied, nodding over her shoulder towards the procession of cops.

"Huh—not here for us... They're... Oh shit. Your parents?"

"I didn't call them, did you?"

"Nu-uh. Priscilla wouldn't have—and the police report to her anyway. The chief is married to her after all."

Ella stared. "Wait, *what?*"

"I thought you knew. Yeah. Priscilla kept her own name, obviously. But her husband, Matthias Baker? The football quarterback, remember him?"

"Dumb and good looking. Smelled like apples."

"Yeah, him."

Ella bit her lip. "Sorry," she said quickly. "I'm—I'm sure he's very smart, I don't know why I said that."

But Brenner was shaking his head. "Nah, you meant it. And you're right. Baker *was* dumb. Dumb as a box of rocks. But his dad was on the force, and in this town, police chief is something of an inherited position." He waved the small brown notebook in his hand towards the cavalcade of cops. "So what's with it?"

Ella shrugged and turned, moving towards the stairs. Brenner followed. As they descended the stairs, she glanced over. "So what's the book?"

"Ledger."

"And?"

"Something's missing."

She glanced up, impressed. "You went through and found some shady numbers?"

He snorted. "Hell no. I mean something's *missing.*" He opened the book and dangled it in front of her. Now she realized what he meant. A large clump of pages had been ripped out of the middle of the book. The tattered, yellowed edges were visible jutting out.

Ella leaned in, taking the book and pausing by the front door. She flipped through slowly, nose wrinkling. "Looks like employee payment records. Baron's on here."

"What's missing?"

"Umm... Everything from last month. All of it. Someone ripped it out."

Brenner tapped his nose. "Aren't you glad you invited me?" he said. He flashed a smile, reminding her briefly of his old self.

She pushed out of the front door, pocketing the small notebook in her coat but then peered up the street towards the large mansion set on the hill. Police were hastening out of their vehicles, racing towards the front door.

They were all stopped, though, as, in the distance, a tall figure emerged, holding out his hands as if to keep back the tide.

"So... we going close or sticking to the nose bleeds?" Brenner asked. He brushed a hand through his blonde fringe, pushing it to the side.

Ella let out a long breath. She knew what she wanted to say. But she also knew she had a job to do. And so in answer, she approached the front seat of the parked SUV. "Thanks for fixing the heat," she muttered.

"Huh? That wasn't me."

She shot him a startled look. But then he grinned. "Nah, just teasing. It was."

She didn't say anything, but that was the second joke he'd made in as many minutes... Some of the sadness had lifted from his eyes. He even sat a bit straighter in the front seat, leaning back, something at ease about his posture.

She wasn't sure what had changed. But at least for a couple of moments, Brenner Gunn looked like his old, cheerful self.

She smiled, but this faded as she turned her attention to her father's home. To the cops surrounding him and the flashing red and blue lights.

Slowly—painfully slowly—she rolled down the driveway and crunched up the fresh gravel road in the direction of her father's mansion.

CHAPTER 9

BRENNER HADN'T TAKEN A sip since the incident with Longstreet. He knew he shouldn't have beaten the man so badly, but he'd learned years ago that if you were going to stand up against a dangerous man, the worst thing you could do was to do it mercifully. Mercy only enraged the bully.

But Longstreet wasn't a bully. The man had lost it for a moment, had tried to strangle Ella. And so Brenner had stepped in. Things in Nome weren't like the lower forty-eight. People solved their own problems, instead of sending every other man off to some hellhole behind bars for walking on a neighbor's yard funny.

Brenner scowled.

He had even shaved, fixed the radiator in her car, fixed the heat and issues with the vents. Hell, he would've changed the oil too if he had thought it would help.

As he shot a glance towards Ella's face, she was wearing a mask again. Every now and then, he glimpsed the truth. The tightness in her lips, the narrowing of her eyes. She was nervous, scared even. But none of this was communicated overtly. In fact, as they rolled down the street, approaching the back of the parked police vehicles, all she said was, "This should be interesting."

For a man who wore his heart on his sleeve, sometimes the understated ways of Ella Porter could be infuriating. Other times, he couldn't help but admire her self-restraint.

And now, they pushed out of the vehicle, moving up the driveway. Three cops stepped forward to intercept them, but Ella's ID flashed in hand. "FBI," she said quietly.

Brenner didn't bother with an ID. He nodded at each man in turn. "Gary, Jacques." He didn't greet the third man; the shortest, wearing glasses. Not because he had anything against glasses, but because he had something against the smaller man. The two of them still disputed it, but Brenner knew the truth. The small man, named Marvy, was a local bookie off hours and when out of uniform. Nothing major and usually only with friends, or friends of friends. But he had insisted Brenner owed him a hundred dollars.

Brenner had never agreed to the bet.

The two hadn't spoken since a falling out at the Lucky Penny.

Grudges in Alaska could go deep, sometimes for generations. Then again, he wasn't sure this was too dissimilar to the lower forty-eight as well. Now that he hadn't been drinking, some of Brenner's usual good humor was returning.

Seven hours without a sip wasn't a particularly *big* accomplishment. Shaving briefly and using some toothpaste wasn't exactly anything to write home about.

But things had been rough in recent years.

And now...

Things were different. There was something... to look forward to? To hope for? To... to...

He didn't know what to think. He shook his head, glancing towards Ella as the small woman moved up the driveway, sidestepping the officers blocking her path instead of trying to push through, turning to avoid the thorns on a tangled shrub embedded in the rough ground on the side of the asphalt driveway. And then she approached the front door where Mr. Porter was speaking to a couple of police officers.

She hesitated briefly, lingering back. Either from nerves or out of a desire to listen, he couldn't tell.

But the first comment from Mr. Porter was enough to snare everyone's attention.

The tall man was wearing a luxurious, red bathrobe. He had knotted it twice for modesty's sake. The man's features were sharp, clean-cut and shaven. He had silver hair neatly arranged. He smelled vaguely of sandalwood aftershave, which Brenner detected even standing behind the nearest officer facing the doorstep.

Mr. Porter had one of those faces that wasn't *just* handsome, but it was handsome in the sort of way that seemed larger than life. The sort of handsome that belonged in a movie or a political ad. The man, even in his bathrobe, also wore a gold watch on one wrist. His slippers were velvet, and his reading glasses, tucked in his robe, looked expensive.

Everything about the man communicated wealth, sophistication and prestige.

Everything except for his trembling voice. The desperation with which he said, "I don't know *where* she is. We retired early tonight. But I woke up ten minutes ago, and she was gone! That's why I called you, Schmidt. Now are you going to do your job or *what*?"

Officer Schmidt raised a consoling hand. "I'm very sorry sir. I know this is frustrating, but we need to know *everything*. When did Mrs. Porter go missing?"

Ella couldn't help herself now. She stepped forward, stunned. "Mom's missing?"

Everyone turned to look at her. "Priscilla," said Schmidt, nodding politely and stepping back.

But Mr. Porter's eyes narrowed. He stared at his daughter. Then, his voice suddenly cool, collected, as if turning on some hidden feature, he said, "Ella. Good to see you, dear."

Ella just stared at her father. "Mom's missing? When?"

Mr. Porter blew some air through his lips. But his demeanor had shifted. He no longer seemed worried or frightened, but now he seemed in control, calm. He adjusted his sleeves, straightening them briefly. "I'm sure it's nothing," he said slowly. His eyes found Schmidt again. "And I'm sure," he said, stressing this sentence, "We'll find out what happened sooner rather than later. Roscoe is missing from his kennel. Lois must have just taken him for a walk. Roscoe *was* barking up a storm earlier this evening."

Schmidt was quickly typing something in his phone, taking notes from Mr. Porter's comments.

But Ella just stared at her father, stunned. Brenner glanced past Mr. Porter, into the luxurious home. No sign of movement. Just a massive, empty house behind the single solitary figure of Ella's father.

Brenner had experienced his fair share of discomfort in Mr. Porter's living room on more than one occasion. He'd always known Ella's parents had hated him. But it didn't give him any satisfaction to know that Mrs. Porter was missing.

Ella had turned now, pointedly ignoring her father, but she was issuing instructions at a rapid pace. Pointing at one officer then the other. She didn't command, her voice didn't crack like a taskmaster's whip. But she did hold up her FBI badge, in an effort to fend off any protests.

She reminded him of some of his commanders back in the Navy. Ella's back was turned to her father, but finally, she was forced to face her old man.

She stared at Mr. Porter, her hands tense at her sides. Everything in her posture screamed discomfort, and yet it was with her ever-calm voice that Ella said, "How long has she been gone?"

Something flashed in Jameson Porter's eyes as he stared at his long-lost daughter. But neither of them mentioned it. Neither of them said a word about their history.

Instead, Porter simply snapped, "Ten minutes. Now do something about it."

Ella nodded; she turned, gesturing for Brenner to follow. He fell into step as she hurriedly moved down the sidewalk, picking up the pace in an effort to leave her father behind her.

Brenner kept his voice low as they hastened alongside each other. "Are you good?" he said.

She nodded stiffly.

Lying again.

But Ella didn't slow, maneuvering rapidly up the street, away from the house. Other officers spread out around them, heading in various directions, following Ella's issued instructions. "So," Brenner said carefully, his breath expanding in the dark. "What's the plan?"

He kept up with her rigorous strides, her smaller legs having to move double time to outpace his lankier gait. His hands were jammed in his jacket pockets, and his cheeks stung. Brenner felt the outline of his sidearm at his hip.

The one solace he'd often found from the demons that came in memory, the pain that still lingered in his mind, had been a simple one.

The shooting range.

It had started *long* before joining up.

Brenner pressed his fingers against the outline of his weapon on his hip. One thing could be said about his life, and it was that he had often missed the target. But the same couldn't be said at the shooting range.

He didn't miss. Of course, Ella didn't know any of this. She didn't know that he had served as a sniper for the most elite fighting force in the country. She didn't know that he spent, at minimum, four hours a day practicing his trade, expending bullets and blasting targets to pieces.

There was a comforting weight about the gun on his hip like a piece of himself. But that was the problem with this sort of work. As a US marshal, and one of the only ones assigned to the small town, his job description did not entail solving crimes. Mostly, he was involved in hunting down fugitives who thought they could make it rich in the gold-mining town.

But now, as he moved through the cold night, in the luxury subdivision, watching Ella out of the corner of his eye, he knew that if he wanted to be of any help, he would have to do things her way. Sometimes, he missed the battlefield. Things were easier. Bad guy there. Good guy here. Shoot that way.

It wasn't always that simple, of course, but he had never been involved in high command. More often than not, he had been left on a dusty hilltop, or lodged on some tall roof, keeping an eye on his team.

One thing Brenner prided himself on, more than anything: in the five years he had served with the SEALs, not a single one of the team members he had been overwatch for had ever died. It was considered the longest streak for a combat-active SEAL team to go without losing a member.

They had even given him some stupid medal for it. More than once, Brenner had taken dangerous shots to preserve his men. Sometimes, though he hated the nickname, they had called him Guardian Angel. Others, a bit less reverently had jokingly referred to him as Greased Lightning. And still others had combined the two names, creating the worst of the bunch. Greased Angel.

In some ways, the Navy had been his happy place. Working on trucks, working with his hands, fixing vehicles, and then heading out on missions, sniper on his shoulder, spotter at his side.

It didn't matter how many bad guys he had shot. All that mattered to him was that none of his team members came home in body bags.

And that had all lasted for years. He had once believed, foolishly he now realized, that maybe it would go on forever.

But then everything had changed. After the incident, he had been quietly discharged. A medical release, they had said. But a very clear connotation, and he could still remember his commander's furious face, spittle flying as he had screamed at Brenner. "You're lucky I'm not court-martialing you. You're lucky I'm not putting your ass behind bars for the rest of your life!"

His commander had never yelled at him like that before. It had reminded him of his father.

Of course, the commander was now dead, hit by an IED. But Brenner's father was still very much alive. If one thing could be said for Mr. Gunn, that asshole wouldn't kick it. Brenner believed the man stuck around just to be mean.

Ella was pointing ahead through the dark now, her voice suddenly shaking. "What's that?"

Brenner spotted it too, tucked along the side of a bike path, near disheveled earth where another house was currently being erected. The ground was muddy, stacks of lumber wedged against the already erected paneling under sheets of plastic to protect the wood from the elements.

But Ella was indicating a small, football-sized lump on the side of the road.

The two of them approached the item, staring at the ground.

Ella went still.

Brenner winced. "I think that's Roscoe."

Ella dropped to a knee, reaching out and touching the small animal. The dog's collar shifted as she reached for the clinking metal nametag. A big, swooping R etched in gold. The address for the Porter family residence.

The dog definitely belonged to Lois Porter...

"Is he breathing?" Brenner said quietly.

Ella looked up; her expression shell-shocked. "No," she murmured. "The dog's dead." This declaration was bad enough—Brenner had a soft spot for dogs. He had two of his own—both rottweilers. A misunderstood breed in his opinion. Loyal and sometimes aggressive—two traits he valued.

But Roscoe's limp body was also an indication of something else.

Where was Mrs. Porter?

"The leash is over here," Ella said, hastening further up the sidewalk. She pointed at the ground. A long, pink, leather lead had been smooshed into the mud. By the looks of things, a truck had been this way.

"See the tread?" Brenner said grimly.

"Yeah..." Ella exhaled slowly, holding her breath for a moment, and then she looked at him. There was a haunted look to her eyes. The look of someone struggling to hold it all together, but—by sheer force of will—somehow managing to keep everything intact, if only for a moment longer.

"I think someone kidnapped my mother."

CHAPTER 10

ELLA SAT IN THE passenger seat this time, staring out the window, watching as they rolled past another rest stop. They'd already been to gas stations throughout the mountains. A helicopter had been deployed by the marshal service. Other police vehicles had been sent to scour the rest of the town. News bulletins were flashing on digital displays. Text messages had been sent out to the locality.

None of this had been done for Baron Jones.

She could still remember the nearly empty crime scene. The coroner hadn't even gotten there for hours after Baron's body had been discovered. Baron was a nobody in Nome. Just like most folk.

But now that Janice Longstreet *and* Lois Porter had gone missing, a state of emergency had been declared. A dead laborer? Nothing much to mention.

But two aristocrats missing? The city was in an uproar.

And Ella found her own emotions warring. She frowned at a truck on the side of the road, near the rest stop. "What about that?" she asked.

Brenner glanced then shook his head. "It's Steven Adams'. We saw him back at the gas station. He sometimes leaves the truck if the battery dies."

"I want to see anyway."

Brenner shrugged and guided their SUV along the side of the poorly maintained road, over fissures and cracks in the asphalt, and then slid into the rest stop. He pulled alongside the motionless truck. Ella hopped out, moving hurriedly. She glanced through her window into the back seat.

Scattered bottles here and there.

But otherwise empty. No sign of a disturbance. No sign of... *remains.*

Ella shivered, staring out across the desolate highway, over the mounds of snow. In the distance, she spotted blue lights flashing off windows as police cars hastened in every direction.

She remembered what she'd been told about Cilla. Her sister was married to the fresh-faced police chief. The police chief's mother-in-law was missing.

The queen of Nome had vanished.

Ella cursed, turning back away from the truck, hopping into the SUV and waving a hand. "Drive," she said. "Please."

"You got it. We still just checking remote spots for a truck?"

Ella shook her head, her breath fogging the window at her side. Brenner's window was cracked, despite the temperature. He seemed to like having the cold wind blow through the car while also keeping the warm air pumping through the vents.

"Three dead people," Ella said slowly. "Two found at the bottom of the sea. Another one killed above their burial site... Was someone trying to hide the bodies?"

"Could be."

"It was on Revcot land, right?"

"Yeah. Five million dollar claim."

Ella hesitated, frowning. "Was it bought or leased?"

"Long-term lease."

Ella shook her head, desperately cycling through her options. The Revcot was considered one of the wealthiest coastal mining locations. And that was where the bodies had been found. Which left the question—who'd buried the bodies there?

She nibbled on the corner of her lip in a nervous gesture, her features stretching into a frown. She leaned back, head against the cushioned chair, and she let out a long, exhaling breath, trying to find some amount of solace by simply closing her eyes and letting the darkness assuage her.

"Who owns the Revcot, then?" she said quietly.

"Tom Dilahunty," said Brenner. "Some hotshot finance guy from New York. He moved here with his family seven years ago. Came here clean-shaven but now he has this big ol' beard. After your time."

Ella snorted. "*My* time," she murmured, shaking her head.

She tried to see the humor for what it was, but her anxiety was spiking, her fear bruiting through her system. Her own mother was missing. Ella didn't even know what to think of that. She hadn't spoken to her mother in twelve years. Hadn't spoken to anyone in her family since she'd left Nome. She'd left and never looked back.

But now... all hell was breaking loose.

"What if... What if I have something to do with it?" Ella said suddenly.

Brenner was still driving, pushing the speed limit. He seemed to like going fast in machines. His injured leg had slowed him down at a dead sprint, but snowmobiles and SUVs weren't nearly so limited. He kept his hand steady on the steering wheel as they picked up pace through the night, moving on a long stretch of road along the coast, heading towards another refueling station near a crabbing dock Brenner had told her about.

"You're saying *you* have something to do with it?" Brenner said, shooting her a sidelong glance. The way the glow of the headlights reflected off the road and caught his features gave Ella a small little pulse of... of something. Nostalgia? Regret?

Brenner Gunn really was the handsomest man she'd ever met. In the right light, he looked like that actor who played in those comic book movies—the lightning god with the hammer. She couldn't remember his name. Chris something. But while Brenner was pretty, he was also sad. That's what he looked like to her. Equal parts of both. Or perhaps entirely both.

She looked away. "No, I'm not saying I had anything to do with it. I'm saying what are the odds that my mom is kidnapped the day I return? I've been gone a decade."

"Twelve years, but who's counting."

"Yeah. Who... maybe that's a good question." Ella wrinkled her nose, drumming her fingers against the steering wheel. She thought of the Revcot claim. Thought of the way the nozzle had been moved under the water.

She also thought of the Longstreet residence. All employee records ripped from a notebook a month ago. The room upstairs with no carpet, no books on the shelves. *The Great Gatsby* on the nightstand.

What did it mean?

They'd killed her mother's dog and taken Mrs. Porter.

But who was *they*?

She gave a long, shaking exhale. "We need to speak with Mr. Dilahunty," she said. "Whoever buried those bodies on his land is responsible for Baron Jones' murder. Also probably behind Janice

Longstreet's disappearance." She drummed her fingers again, feeling a nervous energy rising within her. "Another thing," she said softly. "Whoever took Janice was a diver. He knew what he was doing. Cut the lines. Offed the pump. Moved the nozzle."

"So not just a diver. A miner," said Brenner.

She looked right at him. "Yeah... yeah, you're right. A miner!" She beamed suddenly. "Yes! A miner..."

"So what does that mean? We still speaking to Dilahunty?"

"Yeah. I mean, if he really is the owner of the Revcot, he might know why we've found three bodies on his land. Yeah, that's the next step. And Brenner. Go fast. Okay? Mom's missing."

"Right on it."

Ella leaned back, her stomach in her throat as Brenner pushed the vehicle forward, picking up speed faster and faster, tearing through the night.

CHAPTER 11

THE MAN RECLINED IN his leather chair, puffing on a cigar, his features creased in a frown. He crossed his legs where he leaned back and stared at the three men sitting on his couch. The couch alone had cost more than all three men's cars combined.

He hissed sharply, waving a hand. "Up, up—you've got mud on your pants! Up!"

The men shot upright, shifting uncomfortably and standing awkwardly in front of the red couch. The man took another long puff of his cigar, blowing the smoke out the window at his side. A faint beeping red light showed where the alarm had been disengaged on the window. He'd have to remember to reconnect once he was done.

Especially after everything that had happened.

His fingers tapped against his leg where his pistol rested on his lap. An old-fashioned revolver. A six-shooter. The same type his grandfather had once used to kill a charging black bear.

Sometimes, in the north, things had to be settled the old-fashioned way. Making friends with the bear wasn't an option. He'd tried it already.

The man wrinkled his nose, blowing smoke again, his face cast in shadow, a light behind him illuminating his head with a dull, orange glow.

"Do you think you can handle it then?" he asked slowly, eyeing each of the three men in turn.

Rough men. Muscled men. The sort of men who brawled and drank and bedded. The sort of men who had built the north—had built, with calloused hands—places like Nome.

His home.

Mr. Porter had no doubt that *he* wasn't such a man. The only callouses his fingers had were from scraping through the clean-up after a particularly impressive gold haul. Or perhaps from writing checks and signing contracts.

But it was the way of life on a wild frontier. Someone had to direct the calloused hands. Someone had to be in charge, didn't they?

The Queen of Nome. That's what some called his wife. And now she was missing, and he had a pretty good idea who'd taken her.

"Do you think the three of you will be enough?" said Mr. Porter, pausing to take another drag from his cigar and blowing the smoke out the window.

Two of the men, shifting uncomfortably, jostled the first, sending him stumbling two steps forward. The three of them were brothers. The Watkins family—each of them as rough and tumble as their father had been. Old man Watkins had been put in prison for homicide. A land dispute.

A lot came down to land.

And Mr. Porter would have bet his bottom dollar that *this* nasty business came down to the same thing. His heart pounded in his chest. In part, he missed Lois. She was an anchor. His Queen. In a way, that made him King of Nome, didn't it?

But in another way, it also reminded him how much Lois *knew*. He needed her back. And these were the men to make it happen.

"Merciless," said Porter slowly. "Do you understand this word?"

The oldest Watkins brother, and the scrawniest, was scratching at his disheveled facial hair. "Yes, er, sir, Mr. Porter, sir," he said, bobbing his head a couple of times.

Porter smiled politely at the stuttering man. "You've worked for the company for a while now, haven't you Elijah?"

"Umm. Yes... yes sir?" Elijah Watkins winced, unsure if he was walking into a trap or not.

This was always part of the fun, though, he'd never admit it to anyone. What was the point of wielding power if you couldn't enjoy it? He liked the way Elijah shifted nervously. Liked the hesitant glances, the fearful shifting.

Power... Most would never know the experience.

It was in his power to make the man flourish or cut him off at the root.

"It's your lucky day, Elijah," said Mr. Porter. "I have a promotion in mind. But you're going to have to earn it. All three of you will."

The two younger brothers, both rounder than Elijah and stupider, leaned forward, listening intently.

"Dilahunty," said Porter simply. "Find out if he's behind this. And do it mercilessly. Is that clear?"

"Yes, sir, Mr. Porter, sir," said Elijah.

Porter smiled, nodding knowingly. "And Elijah, Lee, Brendan," he said, glancing at each of them in turn. They all looked shocked he knew their names. But he knew everyone who worked at his company. More than three thousand employees now, across all ventures. He committed names, birthdays, faces, to mind.

Eleanor, his daughter who'd recently returned, had always had a knack for names and faces. But she'd gotten it from her old man. He knew how much each of these employees made on a weekly basis. He knew how many hours they worked. He also knew how many arrests they'd each had.

Which was why he'd chosen *them* in particular for this little mission.

Employing upstanding citizens was the most short-sighted business tactic he could imagine. Mr. Porter had only *ever* employed a combination of tools. Useful for every occasion.

And on this occasion, he didn't need a gentle touch but a battering ram.

"...If any of this gets back to me," Porter said quietly, "Then I'll take it out on your mother. Is that clear?"

He issued the threat calmly, with little inflection. He wasn't interested in upsetting the men, but simply informing them. It was like the snowfall, like the rain. Inevitable.

If. Then. A conditional.

If winds blow, then the storm will come.

If you implicate me in criminal activity, then I'll hurt your mother.

Simple and straightforward, no room for interpretation. That was always the best business practice.

The Watkins boys all stared at him now, swallowing. He wondered how many times they'd gotten into fights over the excuse of protecting their mother's honor. Men like this would use any excuse to fight. But the threat was the reason he'd brought his revolver with him.

The stick was shown, now came the carrot.

"But I'm sure it won't come to that," he said softly. "I trust you three to do what's needed. And in return? Six ounces. Each of you."

"Make it ten," said Elijah abruptly, finding his tongue all of a sudden.

Mr. Porter studied the man. He then flashed a smile. "Ten. Each. Done. And remember—be merciless. I can't have anyone bringing this back to me..."

Elijah paused, glancing at his brothers. Then, still scratching at that mangy beard of his, the scrawny brother muttered, "What if... What if there's nothing there, you know? What if *she's* not there? What if Dilahunty isn't behind it?"

"He's behind it. If not this, something else," said Porter with a sigh, lowering his cigar now, swirling the smoke inside his mouth and then exhaling half through his mouth and half through his nose. He liked how the flavor changed when he did this—something to do with olfactory glands in the nose.

Porter just shrugged. "Either way, that was an itch in need of scratching. So scratch it."

"Can we bring a couple of buds?" Elijah said.

"Do you need more?"

"Just two other guys," said Elijah. "We won't mention your name."

Porter shrugged. "As long as you get the job done. And remember—if it comes back to me, I don't care from who, it's your mother I'm going after. Not theirs. Whoever you have in mind."

The Watkins shifted uncomfortably again. Porter reached into his pocket, slowly removing a large vial of gold dust. He left it on the chair arm, glancing at it. "Ten ounces that," he said quietly. "With the contacts I have, even going crude, that right there could snatch you sixteen thousand, easy."

All three men stared at the gold on the armrest, eyes wide. Elijah licked his lips then turned to shuffle out, gesturing for his brothers to follow.

Mr. Porter took another long drag of his cigar, resting his hand on his revolver and staring at the small tube of gold.

Such a strange allure from something so small.

A bottle of sand wasn't *so* different on a molecular level. But there was something about gold... as if wired into the human DNA.

It had a way of enticing the eye that few other things did.

He didn't even notice when the door slammed further in the house. He simply puffed smoke, stared at the tube of gold, and briefly, forgot everything else. A smile curled his lips as he leaned back in his chair.

A second later, though, he remembered his wife was missing.

The smile slowly faded; he reached out, pocketing the gold again while still puffing on his cigar.

CHAPTER 12

ELLA STARED THROUGH THE window at the inland mining operation. A fleet of mud-stained diggers lined along white shipping containers. Dozers and dump trucks also lined a large warehouse placed against the coast. The sea-facing, corrugated metal wall was stained with rust from the constant ministrations of a summer-time, salt breeze.

Occasional flickers of light flashed through windows set in the shipping containers, suggesting the metallic rectangular structures were being used as sleeping quarters for the on-site workers.

A large metal fence encircled the compound, and bright, metal signs warned off intruders.

The roads leading to the fence were well-worn with treads from large work vehicles. Ella couldn't help but notice a few trucks line up near an office building placed on the bluff overlooking the frozen sea.

"Big operation," Ella said quietly.

"Yeah, some say it's as big as your father's. Bigger, Dilahunty says. He's a purebred gold miner though. No other business ventures beyond it."

The two of them sat in the dark SUV, peering through the chain link fence and surveying the compound.

"Think we need an invitation?" Ella said slowly.

In response, Brenner pushed open the front door, hopped out onto the muddy road, and stomped over to the chain link fence. He tested the gate, frowned, and then she watched in surprise as—in one swift motion, far faster than she'd ever seen anyone at the FBI manage—he pulled his weapon from his holster and fired twice.

He didn't even glance back as he turned and moved back towards the waiting vehicle.

The gunshots still reverberated in the air. A second later, a padlock fell from where it had been shattered. Then the chain followed with a rattling *clunk-clunk-clunk* sound as it snaked through the gap in the fence and spooled on the muddy ground. The last link of the chain fell as Brenner hopped back into the SUV and slammed the door.

"I got us an invitation," he said wryly.

She pursed her lips, staring at the gunshot lock. And then, she didn't say a word, allowing Brenner to take her silence as permission. Their SUV bounced over the worn trail, following the tread of dump trucks.

A mountain of trailings piled high off to their right along the stripped ground near an old, dry riverbed.

More trailings—coarser material—rested beneath a large conveyor belt jutting out over the cliff. A pile of stones as tall as a three story building was equally wide.

They moved along the trail, staring at the array. "How many ounces do you think they get per week?" Ella said quietly.

"Couple hundred. Per sluicer—and they've got three of those. Three locations."

Ella leaned back, exhaling faintly. "Six hundred ounces?"

"Yeah. Millions per week. Enough to kill for, one might even think."

Ella just shook her head in stunned disbelief, then waved a hand, directing Brenner towards the office building she'd spotted earlier. "Light's still on," she said quietly. "Let's see if anyone's home."

They moved up the trail, hopping over dislodged stones and past muddy machinery. And as they drew near the office building, the front door was suddenly kicked open. A man yelled as he stepped out into the dark, illuminated by a glare of white light behind him. He was wearing boxers and no shirt. And clutched in his hands, the old man was gripping a shotgun.

"What the hell do you think you're doing!" the man screamed. "You think those signs were suggestions!" He raised his shotgun, aimed at the SUV and fired twice.

"Shit!" Brenner yanked the steering wheel to the side. Something exploded, and Ella guessed it was their front left tire.

The vehicle skidded on the mud. Ella was yelling through the window. "FBI! FBI!"

The man in his boxers, carrying a shotgun, had a bit of a beer gut, displayed proudly over his gray underwear. His facial hair went down to his navel in an impressive display. The prospector was also wearing a yellow hard hat, which apparently he'd forgotten to remove when taking off his pants and shirt.

Now, the hardhat-wearing, bearded man was waving his shotgun around threateningly. "Next one goes through your windshield!" he crowed. "Get off my land!"

"We're federals!" Ella yelled through the window. "Sir, please lower the gun." Her own weapon was now in her hand. She gripped it tightly but nearly dropped it. Her worst marks at the academy had involved marksmanship. She'd never been much of a shot. Neither had she ever been a grappler.

One thing Ella shared with her father—the ability to get *others* to do their fighting for them.

Ella had never much relied on this manipulative training. Oftentimes, it had felt as if her father had trained her to be a politician against her will.

Now, though, before Brenner could shoot the man, she pushed out of the SUV's front door, badge raised about her head. "Mr. Dilahunty?" she called out.

The man stiffened, staring at her. "Who's asking?" he demanded, grimacing in her direction and peering at her.

Ella kept her badge raised. "Eleanor Porter," she said stiffly. Her last name sometimes worked like a key in a lock. Other times like a slammed door.

And this time, it seemed to be the latter.

Instead of lowering his shotgun, he raised it again. "Porter?" he snapped. "Hell—I told you Porters what would happen if I found any of you skulking about again. How come y'all just don't listen?"

His shotgun was now pointing towards Ella again.

She tensed, her stomach twisting uncertainly. Her own weapon was pointed at the mud. Words had always been preferable to gunshots.

The reason she'd managed to make it so far at the FBI wasn't because she was the best agent. Nor was it because she was the *smartest* agent. She was smart. Had graduated with honors. Had entered college a couple years early and graduated at nineteen from university.

She was damn lucky, and she knew it. But education wasn't the secret to her closure rate at the bureau. Seventy-two hours without sleep, staking out a small motel just to find the courier who had delivered meth to a killer in Colorado had seemed an easy enough thing. Driving across five states, stopping for a brief, five-minute interview *in person* with a witness who'd refused to speak over the phone, and then driving back had been another instance. She'd driven two thousand miles for a single tip.

Nothing had come of it.

Her old partner used to say Ella just doesn't know when she's beat.

And so she slammed the door and stepped forward, facing the man with the gun.

"I'm Ella Porter," she said softly. "Not Priscilla. I don't much like my family either, Mr. Dilahunty, but my mother went missing tonight. Earlier this morning, three bodies were found on the Revcot. So I hope you can see why we might be here."

Dilahunty stared at her, eyes wide, beard shifting across his chest in a way that made her own skin itch. She took a step towards him. Brenner was hissing at her, but she ignored him.

"Get back, missy," said Dilahunty. "I will blow your pretty head off those shoulders."

She took another step forward, staring directly at Dilahunty. Her expression was pleasant enough. She didn't glare, didn't communicate some battle of wills, didn't give him any reason to be offended.

Save one. She kept walking towards the man with the gun. One step after another. No hesitation, no turning around. No second thoughts.

She always paid attention to details. And this man was a caricature. Brenner had said he'd come from the lower-forty eight. Now, he looked like an old-timey prospector. A banker playing a role.

And bankers didn't shoot people.

At any moment, the shotgun might have ripped her in half.

But she felt adrenaline coursing through her system now. And in the same way she'd felt invigorated beneath the ice before nearly passing out, she felt a bit of pep return to her step.

"I said stop!" Dilahunty screamed. He fired the gun off to the side, causing dirt to scatter.

She didn't even flinch. Instead, she walked straight up to him, looked him in the eyes, then patted him on the shoulder in greeting. "Good to meet you, Mr. Dilahunty. May we speak inside?" She gestured with a small, delicate hand towards the open door. She flashed another million-dollar smile to a man who made millions per week, and then she entered the open door of the office, not once looking back.

Dilahunty muttered a few choice expletives, but then he spat into the mud, grumbled something and followed after her.

CHAPTER 13

ELLA GLANCED AROUND THE cramped office space. Blueprints were stacked on a desk scattered with papers. Maps were pinned to a corkboard against the wall. Dilahunty hastened towards this board and began wheeling it away, turning it to the wall so she couldn't see. One of the small wheels squeaked as he rotated the board to face the opposite direction.

The whole area smelled of mud and earth. The vinyl flooring was streaked with combinations of day-old dust and muddy footprints. As Dilahunty secured the maps on the wall, pointing them away, he finally hastened over to a chair and snatched a pair of pants. As he pulled these on with one hand, he faced her, still wielding his shotgun.

Now, though, he was using it as a bit of a crutch, helping to keep him upright. Brenner had appeared in the doorway behind Ella, and his hand gripped his weapon which angled off towards Dilahunty. Ella quickly held out a palm, making a patting motion on the air.

She was pleased to see Brenner lower his weapon, but he was still scowling. The red rings around his eyes had faded. Enough time had passed now since he'd been drinking back on the ice, but instead of calming him, sobriety only seemed to agitate Brenner.

He was shifting uncomfortably back and forth, glancing between her and Dilahunty.

She glanced at him, gave a quick, encouraging nod, her eyes communicating confidence, an air of *I've got this*. She said, "It's fine. We can be friendly here." She held Brenner's gaze a second longer, meeting those sad, forlorn eyes.

She felt another jolt in her chest at the look there but hastily redirected her attention towards Dilahunty again.

"You're Eleanor?" he said, his voice hoarse. He still hadn't buttoned his pants, and his hairy belly drooped over the waistband.

She forced a quick smile, though, bobbing her head once. "That's right."

"I've heard of you," he said.

"You only came to Nome seven years ago, yes?"

"About eight, but yeah. So what's this about your mom?"

Ella watched him. He was shifting uncomfortably, finally having buttoned his trousers, and occasionally glancing out the window and frowning.

"Is something wrong?" Brenner asked from across the room.

Dilahunty shook his head. "You're a marshal, right?"

"That's right. You got some guys on site you're worried about me meeting?"

"Nah. Most the guys went home. Just one fellow, actually—sticking to the quarters. Marriage troubles." He shrugged, looking away from the window now. "So about the Queen of Nome?"

Ella didn't wince, but she wanted to. Instead, though, she simply replied. "My mother went missing earlier tonight."

A low whistle. "Dead folks on my property. The queen goes missing? You really did bring a storm in with you, didn't you, Eleanor?"

"Call her Ella," said Brenner, and at the same time, Ella said, "Please, feel free to call me Ella."

They glanced at each other, and Dilahunty was now smirking. "Some history here?" he waved a dirty digit back and forth between the two.

Ella dodged the question. "I wanted to know who had access to the Revcot claim, sir."

He frowned. His finger lowered. "No one on my watch."

She nodded. "Isn't it true that land owners are required to maintain surveyance of coastal parcels?"

"I mean, yeah. Well—when I say no one on my watch, I mean no one buried no one down there."

"You're referring to the two skeletons we found."

"I'm not referring to nothing—you are! I'm just minding my own business." He was growing agitated again, and Ella noticed how Brenner stepped into the room. The tall, muscled, ex-special forces operator stepped seamlessly to the side, leaning his blonde head against a window. He'd moved surreptitiously, but she knew he'd done it to get a clear line of sight on Dilahunty if needed.

Judging by how quickly he'd pulled and fired on the gate lock, she didn't think Dilahunty would raise that shotgun again without living at least long enough to regret it.

"I wasn't accusing you, sir," said Ella.

"No, but you're implying it. Your smiling eyes, your... your *words!*" He snorted, waving at her. "Sheep's clothing or not, I smell wolf."

Ella turned away, glancing out the window. "Is there anyone here that we should speak to instead, Mr. Dilahunty? I don't mean to interrupt your night. Perhaps it will be better if we send a unit to pick you up tomorrow morning."

"During the height of sunlight," Brenner added.

Dilahunty snorted. "Threatening my operation? Shit, winters come fast. The ground is nearly frozen anyhow. Most the work around here is clean up."

Ella said, "Do you have any idea who might have wanted to kill Baron Jones?"

"Who?"

"Janice Longstreet's assistant."

"Oh… Yeah—yeah, I heard something about Janice. She's missing too, then? Shit. Two golden ladies gone, huh. And so you come to the new guy in town, is that it?"

Ella shook her head. "It was on your land, sir."

"Land I was leasing the Longstreets."

"Of course. I'm not accusing you of anything."

"No, not with your words. Dammit—I've been here for months. Sixteen-hour days. Gotta get in when the sun is shining. I don't know anything about any of it." He jutted out his shaggy beard defiantly, his hands bunched into fists at his sides now.

Ella shot a quick glance towards Brenner, who shrugged right back.

She hesitated a moment, thinking of that little, brown leather journal she now had in her pocket. She pulled it out, raising it slowly, glancing inside. She looked over the top at Mr. Dilahunty. "Any business dealings last month with the Longstreets?" she asked.

He nodded. "Yeah. That's when they leased the Revcot claim. Why?"

"Because," she said carefully, "all their employee payouts are missing from June."

"Well... talk to Vince about that."

"Vince is in custody."

Brenner cleared his throat.

She glanced back and he gave a quick shake of his head. "He's not?" she said, startled.

Brenner shook his head again. "They cut him loose a few hours ago."

She frowned. Vince Longstreet had contaminated evidence and assaulted a federal. Then again, Brenner had nearly beaten him to death. Things were certainly done different up north.

She was beginning to turn back to Mr. Dilahunty, when she spotted something on the desk. A blue map, rolled out. She frowned at the map, studying it upside down. He noticed the direction of her attention, cleared his throat, and swept the thing off the table, knocking it onto the floor. "Your dad send you here?" he said, suspiciously.

She shook her head, holding up her hands apologetically. "Sorry—I was just curious. That was the Revcot, wasn't it?" She waved a hand towards the ground.

"Yeah... So what?"

She shook her head. "Nothing."

In her mind's eye, though, she pictured the small white tick marks on the blue map. A couple of those marks had been in the same spot where Janice Longstreet had been diving earlier that morning. A coincidence?

As if realizing his deflection wasn't enough, Dilahunty cleared his throat and said, "The Longstreets wanted some advice on where to start. So I gave it. We had our own sediment studies done. Part of the lease deal. They pay me well enough, so I see no harm in giving them some pointers. Plus, I get a cut of everything they take out of the ground."

"What type of cut?"

"Ten percent. Pretty standard."

She whistled slowly. "So you were happy with how business was going with the Longstreets."

"Hell yeah," he rocked his head up and down. "Best leasers I've ever had. They get in, get the gold, get out. Only occasionally stop by for advice."

"When's the last time they asked for advice?"

"Oh... huh. Well, probably last year. But that was while we were still in negotiations."

"So sometime last year, Vince and Janice Longstreet approached you about the Revcot."

"Yeah. Mostly just looking for copies of blueprints to do due diligence. I supplied them. Unmarked of course."

"Of course," Ella said, frowning.

Something had clicked in place with this newest piece of information. Another fragment of the puzzle now slotted home. But what did any of it mean?

The missing pages from June. The Longstreet's lease of the Revcot claim. And now her mother and Janice both missing?

Her brow flickered into a frown, and she gave a little shake of her head, glancing out the window now. She smoothed her expression quickly but nodded out the window. "Were we expecting company, Mr. Dilahunty?"

He snorted. "We? No. How about you?"

But before she could reply, Brenner Gunn turned through the open door and stared at the approaching headlights moving towards them. Two vehicles—trucks by the look of them. And they were picking up speed.

Brenner tensed only a moment, and then he spun around on his heel, screaming, "Get down! Get down, now!"

A second later, a chatter of gunfire erupted from the two approaching trucks. The headlights blared through the windows as Brenner slammed the door and flung himself backward, knocking into Ella and bringing her crashing to the ground.

A second later, bullets ripped through the corrugated metal walls, skipping off the ceiling or sparking against the opposite walls.

Brenner draped one arm over her, holding her low, breathing heavily, tensed. Shouting now from outside. The gunfire paused. And then a loud voice, "Dilahunty, get out here, you old coot!"

Dilahunty opened his mouth to shout something back. The shirtless man was ducked behind his counter, shotgun grasped. As he began to retort, though, Brenner lunged towards him, clapping a hand over his mouth. "Shh," Brenner whispered. "They're fishing for your location. Stay low, stay under the table. Metal walls, so bullets might ricochet. Neither of you move a muscle, got it?"

Ella's elbows pressed against the cold, muddy floor. Adrenaline surged through her body but accompanied exhaustion. She'd once been told that if she lived off adrenaline, it would blow out her adrenal gland and collapse her physically. The gland that pumped adrenaline wasn't the sort that could return or heal itself.

Once it was gone, it was gone. One of her colleagues, she'd known had worked sixteen-hour days for *months*. Even years. He'd been fast-tracked to take over as a Supervising Special Agent. But in the end, he'd collapsed. Suffering a nervous breakdown. They'd said he'd shot his adrenal gland, that he'd been running on borrowed energy and caffeine to the point of collapsing his body, his nervous system.

The last time she'd seen him, he'd been crying in a hospital bed, unable to move, unable to rise. The tears had been from sheer exhaustion.

Nothing his body did was able to replenish the same levels of energy, and now, three years later, he hadn't improved much.

She couldn't imagine laying in bed for three years, suffering a nervous breakdown.

But she also didn't know how to calm herself when the adrenaline started pumping. She lay under the table, tense, her own gun clutched in one hand.

The sound of gunshots had faded now. Brenner was standing near a window at the back, shoulder against the wall, occasionally casting his profile in the lights through the windows. Then, he raised his gun and fired twice.

Both shots took out the bright lightbulbs inside the office. The sound of tinkling glass striking the table, the floor.

And now darkness fell. Ella shivered, huddled under the desk. She could feel Dilahunty shifting next to her, the sound of his shotgun scraping the floor. The sound of gunshots had receded to whispered voices. Footsteps.

By the sound of things, men were now circling the office. Once they did that, things would deteriorate quickly. Ella's phone was in her hand, and she was rapidly dialing the police while simultaneously shielding the device with her body to hide the glowing screen from anyone who might see it through the window.

But she knew as well as the attackers did—the police would be too late. Any available cops were already out and about, searching for the Queen of Nome.

This mining site was too far from the coast. No... there would be no time. The best the cops could do would potentially be to find the gunmen as they fled their murder scene.

Brenner had clearly reached the same conclusion. He held a finger to his lips as he leaned against the window, peering down at where she hid under the table.

A sudden rattling sound. The door handle was being turned.

Brenner stiffened, and Ella pointed. The door slowly opened and then *Bang!* A loud blast in Ella's ear.

She was flung sideways, terrified but suddenly realizing the shotgun in Dilahunty's grip was pointed towards the opening door. Pellets had blasted through the door, turning it to sawdust. And through glimpses of perforated wood, she spotted a dark figure cursing, retreating and stumbling. Clearly injured.

The door remained a couple of inches ajar.

"How many are there?" Dilahunty whispered.

"I counted four voices," Ella whispered back.

"Five," said Brenner equally softly. "The one to the northwest hasn't fired yet. He's trying to flank."

Ella stared at the ex-soldier. He was tense now, every muscle braced, it seemed, where he leaned against the wall.

"If we let them surround us," Dilahunty began, his voice trembling.

"Just stay low," she said softly. "We'll be fine."

Brenner shot her a look then seemed to reach a decision. "Stay here. Don't show yourselves."

"And what are you going to—"

His gun raised, he fired twice through the window. The first bullet smashed the glass. The second caught someone who emitted a scream of pain. A third shot cut the scream short.

More yelling from around the front of the office trailer. The sound of footsteps. Brenner didn't hesitate though.

One shot smashed the window. A second shot hit a target. A third shot neutralized the target. And then, in a surging motion, he flung himself through the window, even as the glass continued to scatter.

Ella stared, wide-eyed.

Dilahunty was cursing beneath his breath. She remained hidden under the table, her own gun held in hand. Brenner had told her to stay put... but she *had* trained for moments like these. Gun battles weren't her forte, but she knew how to point and click.

And so she emerged from the table, cautious, careful, weapon in hand. She approached the window facing the back where all the dozers were gathered.

The silence was interrupted by another chatter of semi-automatic weapons.

Two more gunshots from a pistol. The chatter went quiet.

"Where is he?" someone was screaming. "Riley—they got Riley!"

"Elijah!" Another shouted. "Get back—holy hell, he's in the dump truck. Right there! Hit him! Now!"

More gunshots. More screaming. The sudden burst of bright lights reflecting off dark glass as bullets perforated windshields, smashed bumpers, exploded wheels. The dozers and dump trucks were ripped to shreds.

All the while, Ella's heart pounded horribly. "Stay down, sir," she whispered towards Dilahunty. The man had been peeking behind the table, but at her advice, he ducked.

Good thing, because a second later, a crater the size of her fist burst through the wall above his head. Another blast and another hole gouged through the metal.

A twelve-gauge with armor-piercing slugs, by the look of it.

Ella winced, keeping pressed against the wall, and desperately searching through the window for something to shoot at.

She spotted the man with the twelve-gauge hiding behind a stack of wood pallets. No clear shot. He wasn't looking to fire, but rather raising his gun over his head, aiming recklessly and pulling the trigger. Another piece of the wall was ripped out, allowing night air to stream through the trailer.

Ella aimed through the window Brenner had shattered, and she fired twice. One of the shots clipped his cover, the second scored a white mark in the wood, sending splinters flying. The man behind the stacks of wooden pallets ducked low, cursing.

She watched as two more men approached the dozers, aiming at the front cabin of one of the vehicles.

But as they drew close, guns pointing in the windows, Brenner emerged from the dozer to the left. She wasn't sure how he'd duped them. But he fired twice.

One for each man. They went down before they'd even had a chance to aim.

Then, Brenner looked across the dirty terrain.

"Ella, down!" he yelled.

She'd been watching Brenner too closely, and she realized a second later, the man with the twelve-gauge was trying to aim at her, rising slowly from along the side of the wooden pallets. Her own gun whipped around. The twelve-gauge aimed.

Bam!

Brenner shot from a hundred yards away, striking the gunman dead. The twelve-gauge hit the ground—the man carrying it followed a second later.

Ella breathed heavily, listening, frozen in place. No further sounds of gunfire. No sounds of footsteps, nor voices shouting instructions at one another.

But it wasn't until Brenner raised his hand, his thumb jutting skywards, that she breathed a sigh of relief. She shot a quick glance towards the mine boss beneath the table. "Are you okay?"

"Fine, fine. Where's your friend?"

"He's heading back towards us."

"He took all of them out on his own?"

Ella winced and nodded once. "I guess he did."

They both lingered in silence. A few seconds later, a voice called into the trailer, "I'm coming in. Don't shoot."

Brenner stepped into the office space, breathing heavily, his weapon holstered now. He glanced at the two of them and then exhaled in relief. "You guys okay?" he said, double-checking the testimony of his eyes.

Ella nodded once. The mine boss beneath the table remained where he was, muttering darkly beneath his breath.

"What the hell was that about?" said Brenner, scowling. His shooting hand was twitching against his thigh, tapping rhythmically.

Ella stared at the hand motion. She wasn't sure what she should say. She considered her options and then settled on, "Seems obvious enough that someone wanted Mr. Dilahunty dead. They were shouting his name, weren't they?"

They both turned towards the man beneath the table. Brenner took a few steps into the office, reached out, and pulled the table to the side, revealing where the mine boss was still crouched, hyperventilating. He looked up, angry. "Get the hell out!" he shouted.

"I'm pretty sure I just saved your life," Brenner said. "Which means you owe me a couple of answers. Who were those guys?"

"Ask her."

Ella tensed. "Excuse me?"

Now, the mine boss was rising to his feet, breathing heavily and shaking his head in frustration. "I can only think of one person who would send gun thugs to take out the competition. I'll give you three guesses at his name."

Ella massaged the bridge of her nose. "You think my dad sent them?"

Dilahunty spat to the side. "I know it," he snapped. "I'm calling the cops. They'll sort this mess out." He hurried over towards the stack of papers, shuffling them around, searching for his phone.

Brenner was tapping his fingers on his holster, adjusting his coat. A sheen of red stained his sleeve.

"Ella?" he said.

She shot him a look, blinking a few times, feeling as if her thoughts were somewhat delayed. She yawned now, exhaustion replacing panic, replacing surging adrenaline. All she really felt now was tired.

"Hmm? Thanks, Brenner," she said softly. "Nice aim."

He snorted. "Whatever. We're going to have to talk to your dad. You know that, right?"

Dilahunty had finally procured his phone and was muttering angrily as he dialed. Ella stared at the man a moment and then exhaled, turning back to look at Brenner.

"I know," she said quietly. "I was hoping to avoid it. But if anyone's involved in all of this, it's him."

In the distance, she heard the sound of sirens. The police approaching up the long, straight shot road from Nome to the mine's location.

She watched the lights from the police cars dance under the dark sky. She allowed herself another yawn, feeling so very, very tired.

Brenner was curling and uncurling his hand, as if testing his fingers.

"We should give our report," Ella said, wearily. "Maybe help identify the bodies then head back and speak with my dad. That work?"

Brenner met her gaze, held it, then nodded a single time.

CHAPTER 14

ELLA'S EYES FLUTTERED, AND she felt the urge to doze off, her head dipping low then rising again. She stifled a yawn, pressing her head against the cold window in an effort to jar herself to consciousness, but it was no use.

She'd evaded sleep for so long, now it had come looking for her.

Brenner was driving again and looked alert.

Ella sat up straight, forcing her eyes open. Forcing her mind to focus. She even reached up and surreptitiously pinched at her cheek, twisting painfully until some of the pain jarred her senses. She blinked a bit and then rolled down the window, allowing the cold, frigid air to rush through, massaging her face, sending prickles along her skin. The pain, the cold, it would help her keep going. At least for a little while longer.

But the drive back to the luxurious subdivision was a quiet one, with minimal conversation. She shot Brenner a long glance.

He hadn't said a word the whole drive back. He continued to stare out the windshield as if he was watching something painted on the glass—some private movie playing in his mind's eye. Whatever he was witnessing, it wasn't a very pleasant film. He looked haggard, sad.

She felt a pang again. She reached out, her fingers touching his shoulder in the same comforting gesture she'd used with Dilahunty. Except, this time, she really meant it.

"Are you okay?" she said.

"You?" he asked, looking back at her.

"I've seen dead people before," she replied softly. "This morning, in fact."

Brenner sighed, shrugging once.

"You... you didn't do anything wrong," she said quietly. "You were trying to help us. They were trying to kill us."

He blinked, confused, then looked at her, mouth open. "Oh—oh, what? No. No, sorry. I don't give two shits about those guys I dusted. I'm just kicking myself because I nearly missed the asshole by the wooden pallets. He almost had you."

Ella blinked. "Oh... I—I thought you might have been troubled by shooting five men."

"Nah. I'm pissed I didn't shoot that last twerp fast enough." He winced, shaking his head, twisting his hands on the steering wheel. "It was close..." he said, his voice quiet now. "Too close. Dammit."

Ella wasn't sure if she knew how to comfort Brenner. She wasn't sure she *wanted* to.

He was upset because he hadn't shot someone fast enough. Not exactly textbook PTSD.

"You're different than I remember," she said. Instantly, she wished she hadn't. It was the lack of sleep talking, she decided.

He snorted. "Yeah, same with you."

"You've lived a lot of life," she said quietly.

"Well, you knew that when we started dating, didn't you?"

"I... what?"

"Huh?"

"What did you say?"

Brenner just went quiet now.

She frowned at his profile. A very eye-catching profile, but now she felt a flicker of frustration. "What are you going on about?" she demanded. "You keep acting like I'm the one who chose to break up with you... It was twelve years ago, Brenner. We've both moved on. Haven't we?"

"Yeah. Hell yeah."

"Good. So..."

"So, I'll let it go," he said slowly. "Maybe. I guess. I mean what the hell, Ella, just because we weren't dating didn't mean you had to bail on this place!" He was now turning to glare at her, his hand still guiding the steering wheel on the straight-shot road. She looked at him now, and neither of them were watching where they were going.

And neither of them seemed to care. Eventually, this pairing was going to prove a recipe for disaster, she thought. But emotions were hot, and her own tiredness was being quickly replaced by irritation.

"I don't get what you're mad about," she said, refusing to allow her inner turmoil to reveal itself in her tone.

"I'm mad," he shot back, "because you left. You never came back, never called."

"I'm sorry, and I don't mean to beat the same drum, but I should point out again, *you* broke up with *me*," she said, speaking precisely, as if certain he hadn't understood her the first couple of times. In Virginia, a conversation like this would've been completely taboo. They'd known how to dance around office politics, how to avoid sensitive topics. But here? Straight to the point. Twelve years was a long time to hold a grudge.

He just shook his head, turning back to watch the road. A good thing too, because a small, brown creature darted across the ground. Ella stared. "What was that?"

"Wolf pup or something."

"It looked like a wolverine."

"Does Nome have wolverines?"

She shrugged.

Brenner rocked back and forth, biting his lip. "Look, I'll drop it, and I mean to drop it, but why did you leave?"

"Does it matter?" she said, weary again. She also leaned back, her head resting against the cushioned headrest. "This just wasn't the place for me. Things happened. Things changed."

"What sort of things?"

"Everything, Brenner. Look, we used to talk like this. But we don't know each other, not anymore. That's fine."

"Yeah, I guess so."

There was that familiar tone of sadness to his voice now. She felt the same emotion settle on her chest. She released a long, pent-up breath, inhaling the cold air flowing through the open window.

She could still remember what she had seen when she had been sixteen. In the end, it had been the final nail in the coffin. Perhaps it was the exhaustion, perhaps it was just an inability to hold her tongue. And maybe, just maybe, she wanted to know. Didn't she deserve to know?

Perhaps *deserve* was the wrong word. People didn't deserve much of anything from anyone.

Perhaps a better way to think of it was, didn't she *want* to know?

"I saw you with Priscilla," she said softly.

Brenner hesitated. But he didn't ask what she meant. He didn't ask for correction or clarification. He just sat there, somehow slipping further into his chair.

"I saw you two kissing. I know it was after we broke up. But I had already known my family and I weren't cut from the same cloth. And then to see my sister going out with my ex-boyfriend, it just didn't seem right."

She had a quiet, tired smile. She looked at Brenner, shaking her head. "I'm not angry. I promise I'm not. I guess I used to be but not anymore. Still, you keep wondering why. That was partially why. You broke up with me. And then my sister went straight to you. My parents never understood me. And this place, I don't like it. I really don't. I'm not royalty. I don't like being treated like it just because my parents have money."

"I shouldn't have broken up with you," Brenner said quietly. "And with Priscilla, I shouldn't have—"

She silenced him by patting him on the shoulder again. She gave his arm a little affectionate squeeze. It was equal part comforting but also firm. Final. "Let's not," she said simply. "It's over between us. And that's probably for the best. For both of us. That doesn't mean we can't work together. Maybe tomorrow, if you want, you can request a transfer. No doubt Priscilla set this arrangement up just to mess with the two of us."

Brenner swallowed but didn't reply. He just looked sad again. And it was a sadness she couldn't take away. A sadness that existed on the inside, where no one else could access.

And even if she could remove the sadness, that wasn't her role. She wasn't back here to start rebuilding a life she had run away from. She was here for a few months, maybe a year. And if she was able to solve cases, to do a good job, then she would leave again, and even if her job was at stake, next time, she swore to herself, she would never come back.

At least, that's what she had said the first time too. But if it ever happened again, she nodded to herself. This wasn't worth it. She had thought, maybe, she would be able to avoid her family, avoid old connections.

But only the first day back, and she had already seen her family. She was sitting in a car with Brenner.

No, you couldn't avoid your past. Sometimes, that meant it was best to simply run from it.

Her phone buzzed, and she glanced down. Another message from the same number. The unfamiliar number who had said they were a friend and who had texted her back at the motel. *Have any new cases?* the text read.

She frowned at it, her fingers hovering. *Who is this?* she texted again.

And this time, she didn't receive a reply.

She frowned, glancing up from her phone, and looking out across the mountain valleys towards the subdivision. She could just about make out her father's house, wreathed in an orange glow. Brenner spotted it too and picked up the pace, tearing through the wilderness, burdened with snow and racing towards the Porter residence.

Three murdered. Two missing. Gold miners on both sides. The upstairs room at the Longstreet home missing a carpet, the books from the bookshelf. The missing pages from the journal. And what Dilahunty had said about a year before, giving advice about the new claim.

Plus someone had killed Roscoe, the small dog.

The final linchpin, because he loved being the center of everything, would be found back at her father's house. As much as she dreaded the conversation, the confrontation, there was no avoiding it.

Chapter 15

"Come in, come in," her father said, waving them in with a sweeping gesture of his arm. He was wearing a different bathrobe now. Silk with pink and green stenciling up and down the side, displaying ferns and flamingos.

He smelled faintly of cigar smoke—the expensive kind. And he stood in a house about six times too large for empty-nesters. His million-watt smile was out in full display, and he was gesturing at Brenner and Ella as if greeting old friends.

She didn't enter the house but remained standing on the welcome mat on the patio. "No, that's fine," she said politely. "I wouldn't want to intrude."

"No intrusion at all—I don't want you to catch a cold."

She shot back, "I couldn't possibly take up too much of your time. I know you're a busy man."

He smiled back and replied just as firmly, "And you look so very tired. I wouldn't be doing my civic duty if I didn't welcome you in. And honestly, it's quite chilly by the door. Come, come." He made another sweeping gesture.

And like that, he won the exchange.

Because with her father, conversations *always* had a winner and a loser. That was exactly how he liked it.

Brenner had watched the exchange between the father and his daughter with some amount of amusement. He allowed Ella to grudgingly enter the house first, and only then did he follow.

Ella took a step into the house then winced. "I really shouldn't take my shoes off," she said, allowing the door to shut behind her. "My feet are so very sore. I'm not sure I can walk properly without them."

"No worries. Leave them on—just through here. The den is much warmer."

And again, her father won round two. And again, she followed after his sweeping gesture—his bathrobe billowing like a bat wing. Brenner fell into step behind her.

Her father was sitting on a red couch now, puffing on a cigar he'd conjured from an ashtray. He smiled at the two of them as they drew near and indicated a couch across from him. "Have a seat!" he exclaimed.

"Sorry, my knees," Ella shot back.

"It's a very comfortable couch. I'm sure it will help."

But she met his gaze firmly, every ounce of stubborn she'd learned from him now pulsing from her stare. Her lips remained in a quizzical smile, though, nothing about this amused her. "Maybe in a second. Thank you so very, very much for offering."

Her father conceded this round with a small tip of his head.

"So," he said, starting the conversation for them. "To what do I owe this pleasure? Mr. Gunn—good to see you again."

Brenner nodded back. "Porter," he said.

Ella's father gave a smile like a satiated crocodile. He then turned his gaze to his daughter. "And it's been some time, hasn't it? What now, five years?"

Twelve, she thought. "Something like that," she said.

They both exchanged smiles neither of them meant.

Ella remained where she was standing, refusing to sit in the red, leather chair across from her father. Her eyes traveled the floor, and she noted something odd. "The carpet," she said softly, pointing towards the tiles beneath her feet, and then to a rolled-up mat left by the back door. "Someone was cleaning recently?" she asked, glancing up.

Her father's smile didn't slip a single centimeter. "Oh, you know," he said airily, waving his hand. "Your mother is often tidying. You can ask her when you find her. How is that going by the way?"

"We're still looking for her," Ella replied. "The police force is out in full."

"Priscilla's doing, that, I believe," he said with a nod.

"Yes... I guess she is. Is there anything maybe you might not have let slip the first time we spoke? Anything you wanted to bring up now, perhaps?" Ella said carefully. She quickly added. "It was a very emotionally distressing time, I know. No one would blame you for a mistake."

Her father steepled his hands beneath his chin. He hesitated, then his perfectly groomed, silver hair shifted as he looked to Brenner. He gave a little wiggle of a hand towards his daughter. "See how she does that? She's good, isn't she?"

Brenner just shifted uncomfortably.

Her father threw back his head and laughed. "Oh, my dear, dear Eleanor. How I have missed you these last few years."

Twelve years, she thought. But he knew. And he knew that she knew.

He said, "There's nothing I've held back. Why would I? My wife is missing. You should speak to some of the other miners in the area. Vince Longstreet's wife is missing, too, yes? Clearly, a rival is targeting our families. Maybe someone like Calhoune. Or, oh—what's his name. Dilahunty. The new guy. Have you spoken to either of them? Or what about Mrs. Clarke. Sussanah has had ambitions in the past." He shook his head, clicking his tongue.

Ella watched him, glanced at the rolled-up carpet to the side of the door, her eyes narrowed now. The exhaustion was doing funny things to her inhibitions. Or perhaps it was simply being back here—this was a new home compared to the last time she'd been in Nome. It was disorienting, facing a man she had tried so hard to escape.

"You never did let me get that tattoo," she said softly, her expression unreadable.

"I—what?"

"The tattoo I wanted. Right here, on my wrist." She pulled back her sleeve, exposing bare skin. "I never did get it. I couldn't say why, but I didn't."

Her father just blinked at her. "I'm afraid I don't understand."

"It was because you were worried how it might look in a photo-op. That's why you wouldn't let me get the tattoo. You were concerned about the business."

"Are you... accusing me of something, dear?"

"No. I'm saying that Mother's disappearance wouldn't be enough to get you to tank the thing you've built. Your true love, Dad."

"And what is my true love, Eleanor?" he said, his tone amused.

"Porter Enterprises," she said without missing a beat.

"Well, you certainly do have an imagination. You always did, of course." His tone remained the same, but he was leaning forward a bit now, blowing some of the cigar smoke towards where they stood rather than back out the window. His arms folded, and the skirts of his silken robe shifted. Ferns and flamingos arched over his raised knee.

"Everything I've built, dear, everything was for your mother and our children. Is that why you're back?" he said, dropping his voice to a stage whisper and wincing apologetically. "Are you out of cash? I can write you a check, right now!" He surged to his feet and took three long strides towards a desk under the window, illuminated by the moon.

An ashtray rested on this desk. He snatched a checkbook from the table, fluttering it like a fan, and then procured a pen. "How about ten thousand dollars, would that help, dear? Hmm? No—what about a hundred thousand? A quarter of a million? That's a nice sum. I could give you one of these houses. You could live down the street. That car you're driving looks somewhat worn. Hopefully, the heat is working. I could get you another car. Five cars... Any and all of it is yours, Ella. All you have to do is ask. I want nothing more than to help you, dear. I have always loved you and Priscilla equally. Even after these few years of separation."

Ella stared at her father, feeling her heart pound. She had seen him sign checks before. It was the most painless ceremony of enslavement she ever had seen. It was amazing the sorts of things people would do for a slightly more comfortable life. Her mother had loved the deal, too. Ella could picture the Queen of Nome in her mind.

Lois Porter was just as tall as her husband, and also five years older but there had never been any sign of age in her hair—this was due in large part to copious amounts of dye. But on top of it, she also had very few wrinkles. Though Lois had been in her mid-forties when Ella had left, the woman had looked like she was possibly in her late-thirties. And a *gorgeous* late-thirties at that.

Money bought power, but it could also buy youth... of a kind. What it never seemed capable of imbuing was anything recognizable as love.

Ella exhaled faintly, keeping her temper in check. "No, thank you. How very kind of you to offer, Dad."

"You're sure?" he said, tilting his silver eyebrows. "I'm feeling generous tonight, Ella."

"I see... Would it matter to you to know that the small hit team sent against Dilahunty failed? Do you still feel generous now?"

This time, there was nothing thinly veiled about the inference.

Her father's eyes flicked up, over the checkbook, his gaze moving from her to Brenner and back. "What are you talking about? Someone attacked Dilahunty, too? So I am right!" He straightened now, ballpoint pen still clutched in hand and brandished like a conqueror's sword. "Someone is targeting the gold families."

"It looks like it," Ella replied quietly.

She shot another look towards the rolled-up mat. She then exhaled briefly. There was nothing on her father. She doubted anything would be traced back to him. She waved a hand towards the door where the rolled-up mat was leaning. "You have a camera in the back, right?" she said quietly. "Mind if we see that footage? You know. For the case."

"Oh, I wish I could. The camera in the back has been a bit on the fritz."

"So no one would see if anyone came up the garden path through the back gate, hmm?"

"I guess they wouldn't. Is that where they came, do you think? Is that how they took your mother?"

Ella stared at her father a bit longer. And then she gave a little snort of amusement. "You never cared about mud."

"Pardon?"

"You never cared about mud. But she did." Ella pointed towards the ground. "You were trying to get her back your own way, weren't you?"

"I really don't know what you're rambling about, dear. Is this how they taught you to do it in those big, fancy cities down south? I... I mean... You are the expert, so I'll defer, of course. But... well, if there isn't anything else."

"What are you going to do, Dad—Dilahunty didn't attack Mom."

"Oh—you're certain of this?"

"Pretty certain. I was there," she said testily, "When five gun thugs showed up and tried to mow all of us down."

He looked startled. His hand darted to his mouth. "Oh, God. I'm so sorry! That's horrible. Did they catch any of the bastards—pardon my language."

Brenner grunted once. "I got 'em."

"Oh, oh, good. Thank goodness. Who was it?"

"They're still identifying the bodies," said Brenner.

"Bodies, plural? How many of them did you shoot."

"Four," Ella said quickly, before Brenner could reply. He was too damn honest to be allowed to answer the question. "We got four. The fifth one is currently in custody. We're actually going to be speaking with him. Down at the station. He says he may want to confess..." Ella smiled sweetly. "I'm optimistic about the outcome."

"I see... And—you'll be speaking with him tomorrow I bet. First thing—I mean, you do look so very exhausted."

Ella nodded. "Yeah. That's the plan. Tomorrow morning. First thing. Don't worry, we'll find out who hired him. We'll find out who's behind all of this, dad." And then she gave him a polite little nod and turned on her heel, moving towards the door.

Brenner fell into step. As they moved out front, the door shutting behind them, Brenner began, "What was that—"

She turned sharply, looking him in the eyes. "Sorry," she said, loud enough for the small security camera over the door to pick up. "I shouldn't have told him about the survivor. But he just makes me so mad, sometimes. We're scheduled to interrogate him at first light, yes?"

Brenner blinked. His brow furrowed. He was too honest of a man to even realize the intent of the deception. In a way, this was endearing. And in another way, it was downright infuriating.

She gave him a long look, her head twitching ever so slightly towards the camera over the door. And finally, it registered. "Oh... Okay," he said, cautiously, scowling.

And he said nothing further, likely tweaked by his conscience. Brenner always had exhibited an over-active conscience growing up. At least in certain things; stealing, lying, cheating, gossip. He refused to participate.

Then again, shooting five men who were threatening someone he'd grown up with? He wouldn't lose a wink of sleep over it.

She thought it a minor miracle Brenner's father had lived all these years. She supposed it was fortunate for Mr. Gunn that his son hadn't started military training until *after* Mrs. Gunn had died of cancer. Because otherwise, she couldn't see the old, mean-eyed man living through another outburst against his wife and only son. Brenner had stood up for his mother as a kid, for years, taking much of the abuse on himself instead.

No child should ever have had to endure that. Ever.

Brenner had fought back... But nowadays...

She didn't think he'd fight the same way. At least... after a fight, she didn't think there'd be another. Yes, she decided, Mr. Gunn was lucky he was still alive.

Brenner's door slammed shut as he slipped into the front seat. Ella glanced back at the door to her father's house, frowning briefly. She refused to even look in the direction of the camera. Far better her old man didn't think she knew it was there.

It was a flimsy trap. But if her father *had* hired those five gun thugs, then the idea that one of them was still alive would eat at him. Of course... She winced suddenly, remembering that Priscilla's husband was on the police force.

His first call would be to Chief Matthias Baker. The man she thought of, though more quietly from now on, as dumb, good-looking and smelling of apples from the shampoo he used in high school.

She sighed, massaging the bridge of her nose.

No—the ruse wouldn't work. Her father would know all five gun thugs had been shot. Unless... She knocked on the glass window, and Brenner frowned, rolling it down. "Hmm?" he said.

"I'm going to do something I probably shouldn't," she said quietly. "I just need to know if you'll back my play."

"I... what play?"

"Well... I need to rattle a cage or two."

"So—what play?"

She glanced towards the house, back at Brenner, then winked. Her hand shifted at her hip. Brenner blinked, opened his mouth, closed it. "Shit. Yeah—I've got your back."

She smiled sweetly then turned on her heel.

<h1 style="text-align:center">CHAPTER 16</h1>

Mr. Porter sat in his chair, frowning and puffing on his cigar. Ella was clever but not nearly as practiced as he was in the art of deception. A thinly veiled ruse, of course. Even if he hadn't already been provided a full police report of the crime scene, even if he hadn't already known from his hunting buddy, Dr. Messer, the coroner, that five bodies had shown up in the morgue half an hour ago, he would *still* have known she was lying to him.

Ella always had a tell. It wasn't so much something physical he could describe if asked. But rather an attitude. An atmosphere. A way of *being* she exhibited so strongly.

Too confident. Overacting. She'd even paused on his camera—he'd watched her on his phone. Whispering loudly enough for him to hear... Planting the ruse.

What was she up to? Why was she back in Nome? Some people said that it was because she'd missed home.

But one meeting with her was enough to completely clear this option off the table. He sighed, slowly, and made his determination. He lifted his phone, texting the person he always texted when he needed more information. *Was Ella fired? Why is she here?* He sent the message, staring after it.

Only a few seconds passed before the responding blue text bubble returned.

On it. The message replied.

He smiled, and placed his fading cigar in the ashtray, watching the faint whisper of smoke rise and drift towards the open window.

Ella wasn't half the liar he was, but she was clever. She'd spotted the rolled-up carpet by the door. He'd moved it to avoid letting the Watkins boys track mud into the house and onto the carpet. His wife would have had a fit.

That's what Ella had meant. Perceptive. He had to give her that. She'd known he was the one to speak with the hit team. She couldn't prove it. Especially since Brenner had apparently shot them all.

A useful thing to have a man like that on the payroll. He wondered if the US marshal was looking for a new job.

He'd have to make the offer.

Eventually, everyone had a price. The Watkins boys weren't exactly professionals. But five kills? Impressive. Very impressive. He texted the same number again, this time typing: *Brenner Gunn. Did he serve?*

And then the back door suddenly crashed open. He whirled around, startled, his hand reaching for the revolver he kept in the leather chair.

Ella was standing there, her own gun in hand, pointing at him. "Dad," she said politely. "Sorry for coming in the back. The camera's off, right? Hopefully, I didn't startle you. After thinking about it, Mr. Porter, you're under arrest."

He stared at her, bug-eyed. "You—what?" he snapped.

"Yeah," she said simply. "Arrest. You hired those gun thugs. You went after Mr. Dilahunty."

"Prove it!" he snarled.

"Don't have to, dad. Not to arrest you. I'm the only fed in town. My purview is wide. I'm not in your pocket."

Brenner Gunn slipped past her, handcuffs raised.

"You have no authority here!" he yelled, rising angrily to his feet. "Where's Chief Baker?"

"Your son-in-law?" Ella said quietly. "Oh, I'm sure he'll hear about this. Probably... probably in the morning is my guess. We wouldn't want to disturb him so late at night."

"This is an outrage! Ella, think *very* hard about what you're doing here," Porter spluttered, his face turning red, his temper rising.

Brenner grabbed his wrist which had been reaching for the revolver, tugging insistently. He then turned Mr. Porter around, pulling his hands behind his back.

"Ella!" he said, his voice shaking. "Think about what you're doing, dear. Think about it!"

Ella chuckled. "Are you going to threaten my mom, Dad? She's your wife. Good luck. Brenner's mom? She's dead."

"It's true," Brenner said dispassionately.

"Isn't that what you do?" Ella replied quietly. "Threaten the family members of those you want to control? Not going to work with me, Dad. I mean—maybe you could threaten to take out my old man. I might listen then."

He couldn't remember the last time he'd been so furious. All he could see was red. All he wanted to do was reach across the room and throttle that ungrateful little bitch's neck. His eyes bugged as he was herded past his daughter.

As he did, he snarled under his breath, "You *will* regret this."

Ella just watched him leave, and she didn't say a thing. Porter snapped as Brenner pushed him from behind, sending him down the garden path, his bathrobe fluttering. "I demand to speak with my lawyer!"

"We'll sort it out down at the marshal's office," Brenner replied, sounding bored.

"Wait—the marshal's? No—no, hey! You take me to the police station, do you hear me? This is an unlawful arrest!"

"Technically, I'm detaining you until inclement conditions improve and we can transfer you to the police precinct."

Brenner's hand prodded him forward again, up the stone slab walkway, through the metal gate and out towards the idling SUV in the driveway. It was the same route Watkins and his brothers had taken to avoid the cameras.

As he was shepherded forward, Porter snarled, his teeth tight, but he kept any further comments to himself. This was how she wanted to play it, then?

He seethed but forced his emotions to recede, forced himself to calm. Ella had just made the biggest mistake of her life.

And if she kept it up, it wouldn't be a very long life.

He'd done worse things to people he liked better over smaller incidents. He was going to remind her—remind *everyone*—why they called him the King of Nome.

CHAPTER 17

Ella paced back and forth in front of the cold interrogation room, glancing through the one-way mirror to where her father sat, hand-cuffed to the chill table.

Brenner leaned against the glass, watching her instead of the detainee.

"Did you think past this point?" he asked casually, watching her.

Ella stared through the glass. "Hmm?" she said.

He repeated. "Did you think further ahead than this?"

She glanced at him and blinked. "Sorry, what?"

Brenner snorted. "You're beat, Ella. Get some rest."

She glanced back through the glass, frowning. "He's going to be pissed," she murmured quietly. "But I knew that," she said. She frowned. "I just…" she glanced at Brenner. "Does your boss know we've got him here?"

A snort. "My boss lives in Washington State. He doesn't know a thing. Only a couple of others work here—neither is a marshal. I've got the run of the place," Brenner said with a wiggle of his eyebrows above his blue eyes.

Ella returned her attention to her father. The real reason for arresting him wasn't to interrogate him. But because she wanted to go through his phone. She glanced down, lifting the device and studying it, her expression fixed in a frown. "What do you think his password is?" she said slowly.

"I mean… he's your dad."

She tried *LOIS*.

Nothing. The phone vibrated in her hand. She paced back and forth now, in the small surveying booth. The cold, empty marshal's office echoed with silence beyond the open door. She tried again. *CILLA*.

Another vibration.

She tried her father's birthday. Her mother's. She hesitated, biting her lip. Then shrugged and tried *ELLA*.

Nothing.

"Only five tries left, and it locks me out," she murmured.

"What about something related to his business?" Brenner said. "Porter Enterprises."

She snorted. "It would be just like him to use his last name." *PORTER*.

Nothing. Four tries left.

GOLD. Nothing. "Dammit," she said. "I thought that would be it." She frowned briefly, glancing at her father. And then her lips twisted in a faint smile. "Maybe..." *KING*.

The phone opened.

"Ha!" she crowed, shaking the device. "Ha!" she repeated.

The moment she lifted the phone, though, it started vibrating. A soft blinking light flashed from the camera lens. She frowned, staring. She realized the phone's video recording had been prompted. "What's this?" she muttered.

Brenner glanced over her shoulder. "Looks like an app was activated," he said. "Yeah, see there—the green thing. It's—"

"Shit. Facial recognition." Ella winced and stared as the phone suddenly began to vibrate. "What's happening? Dammit—what's happening?"

"Beats me."

She spotted a progress bar as it appeared at the bottom of the phone. The text above simply read *Deleting...*

"No!" she yelped. "It's purging his files!" She cursed and quickly began cycling through the phone. Desperate. As she moved through folders, she watched as—one at a time—the items were deleted, vanishing from the browser.

She cycled to pictures and paused only a moment, staring at an image of Lois and Priscilla smiling at the camera while standing in a ball-room, both wearing lavish, frilly dresses.

Ella stared at the photo only a moment before hastily cycling away and searching desperately through the most recent messages her father had received. But these were vanishing too. She clicked on a message near the top, but before she could read anything, it disappeared.

Muttering darkly, her fingers flying over the phone, she desperately searched for *something, anything* to stop the purging of messages.

But the facial recognition app continued to blink. She should have known her father wouldn't have let his phone fall in the wrong hands. As she swiped down, she paused long enough to notice the heading on a text chain.

VL was the contact name. And the top text simply read, *No deal.*

But then before she could click it, this text message vanished as well. All of it had taken a minute tops. Brenner had been shuffling around for a charger cable and returned with a laptop in hand, breathing heavily, a cable in the other.

"Time?" he said.

She stared at the device—the screen had gone black.

"No..." she muttered. "He deleted his whole damn phone." She scowled, glaring through the one-way mirror.

Her father was leaning back, frowning at his hands, motionless where he was cuffed to the table. Now not only had she pissed off the most powerful man in Nome, she'd deleted his phone.

She bit her lip. "That... that wasn't ideal."

"Did you at least find anything?" Brenner asked hurriedly.

She shot him a look and grimaced. "No. Anything I clicked just got deleted faster." But then she paused, frowning. "VL."

"What?"

"Vince Longstreet. VL. His initials were in a text chain."

"Did you see when it was sent?"

"Sometime last month. It was much lower down the list."

Brenner faced her, tugging the phone from her hand, trying to turn it on then tossing it onto the desk. "You didn't see anything he sent?"

"One thing," she replied. "It said *no deal*."

"No deal?"

"Mhmm."

"So... maybe your dad and Vince were trying to broker something but it fell through."

"Yeah... yeah, that's probably right," she said slowly.

She turned now, her back to the mirror, pacing back and forth, massaging her temples with her thin fingers. "I... Vince had a room at his house. The carpet was missing."

"And?"

"My dad removed the carpet by the back door... he didn't want mud on the ground."

"Mhmm. You were saying that's probably where his gun thugs came into the house. You think someone came in that way to kidnap your mother?"

"Yes," Ella said softly. "And I think I might know who." Even as she said it, she felt a faint prickle along her face. It made sense. In fact, it was the only thing that made sense, didn't it? Unless she simply wasn't aware of all the players involved. She frowned slowly.

"So hang on—what's that about Vince's room upstairs?"

"The books were missing from the shelf. There *used* to be books, by the dust patterns. But they were missing."

"Right... huh. Why get rid of a bunch of books? Think he was researching something naughty?"

"No. I think it's the same reason he got rid of the carpet." Ella crossed her arms, then stared directly at Brenner.

"What?" he said, staring back.

She shook her head, trying to make sense of it. She rocked back on her heels, releasing a pent-up breath at the ceiling.

"You said you know who?" Brenner pressed, frowning at her.

"I said I think I might know who... but..." she peered through the glass at where her father was sitting straight-postured, scowling and facing directly forward, refusing to look side to side.

"Not your old man?"

She tapped a finger against her lips. She was close... she could feel it. But she needed to confirm something. The problem was the black sand—the sediment. The killer, the kidnapper, had been a diver, a miner. He'd known about water lines, had known about the nozzle. But...

Whoever had hidden those skeletons under the ocean had done slipshod work.

She held up a finger suddenly, pulling her phone from her pocket and dialing the number for Dr. Tulip Messer.

She waited impatiently for the coroner to connect. After the second ring, the call was answered. In the background, she thought she heard the laughter of children, the patter of footsteps. Then came a loud guffaw of a laugh—Dr. Messer's voice. "Look at that pudding—that's not where it goes, Malley!"

The chuckling continued but grew louder, suggesting the phone was now being raised to Dr. Messer's cheek. "Hello there," she said.

"Hey, Dr. Messer. This is Ella."

"Who?"

A sigh. "Eleanor Porter."

"Yes! Of course—how are you, Ms. Porter?"

"Ella is fine."

"Sure, sure. Ella. I'm so very sorry to hear about your mother..."

Ella winced. She supposed in a small town like this, *everyone* knew each other's business. Plus, Dr. Messer was the coroner...

A slow chill crept up Ella's spine. "You haven't... there hasn't been..."

"Oh, no, no. No new guests to the morgue. Your father is a hunting buddy of mine—a couple of our friends mentioned it in passing. I'm sorry."

"Yeah. Yeah, that's alright, thank you." Ella glanced towards where her father was still sitting in the interrogation room. She wondered what Dr. Messer might think if she had seen this particular development.

"Is there a reason you're calling, dear?"

Ella was reminded of the grandmotherly face beneath silver hair. The laugh lines and the chocolate chip cookies stored next to the corpses at the morgue. She smiled, finding again that she quite liked the coroner.

"Just a few questions about the bodies."

"Right—I'm still working on things. Had to head home a bit early for my grandson's birthday." Then, she added a bit defensively as if anticipating a rebuke, "I already did three double-shifts this week."

"No, that's fine. Just the two victims?"

"Yes. Both male."

"And no identifications?"

"None yet."

"Could you tell if either..." Ella paused. This was the part she hadn't been sure how to ask. So she just said it. "Had either of the skeletons buried under the water been shot or stabbed before?"

"Before? As in something besides the killing blow?"

"No—something before they were attacked. Is there a way to tell?"

"Oh—well... Now that you mention it, there were a couple of marks in the arm of one of the victims. Could have been gunshots. Hard to tell without any flesh." A sudden burst of laughter. "I see—yes. Here, grammie is on the phone talking about dead people. I'll be right there, okay, cutie?"

Ella waited patiently.

Then the coroner continued, "Sorry—I don't get to see my cutie-pies often enough." She chuckled merrily. "Well, at least twice a week, so not so bad."

"Not at all. I hope I'm so lucky one day..." Ella trailed off, unsure why she'd said this part. It really was getting late. "Anyway, thanks for your time. That's all."

She bid her farewell then hung up.

Brenner was watching her again. He seemed to like doing this a lot. The tall, blonde man had crossed his arms and occasionally stifled a yawn as he spectated. Now, though, he quirked an eyebrow up, his newly shaved chin jutting towards her. "So?" he said.

"I think... I think I know what happened," Ella said carefully. "The two victims under the sea were men. One of them had been shot before."

"So?"

"So... It's rare to get shot unless you've gone looking for trouble."

Brenner didn't reply. His eyes held a distant look for a moment, and she wondered if he was thinking of his time in the Navy.

She quickly said, "Wait here. I just need one more thing confirmed."

"With your dad?" he asked, watching as she moved around the room towards the door that led to the interrogation room.

Ella paused, her hand on the cold handle, shivering as she did. She bit her lip, staring back at Brenner. "I think... I think those two men found at the bottom of the sea worked for my father."

Brenner's eyes bugged. "You think your dad killed them?"

"That's the part I'm not sure about. But I think he employed them. And if I can get him to—"

Suddenly, there was a loud pounding on the door of the marshal's office. Glass rattled, and a voice shouted from out in the night. "I know you're in there, Ella! Brenner! Open this door—*right now*! I mean it. I'll smash this window in. Open! Dad? Dad are you in there?!"

Ella grimaced, staring at Brenner.

"Priscilla," they both said at the same time.

At that moment, another voice called out. A deep, booming voice. "Mr. Gunn! Ms. Porter! This is Chief Baker. Please open this door now—you're both crossing jurisdictional lines now. Let's be reasonable here!"

"She brought her husband," Brenner said, glaring. And something else crossed his expression which Ella couldn't quite place.

But she was still gripping the cold, metal handle of the sealed interrogation room door. "Can you..." she hesitated, wincing. "Can you keep them at bay, please?"

Brenner looked at her, sighed, then nodded once. "I can do that."

"Just for a few minutes, okay? Stall them."

"I won't lie," Brenner said.

"I never thought you would. Now please—go!"

Gunn shrugged then pushed through the second door, leading back into the office space. Over a couple of cramped desks and a single coffee pot set on an empty table, Ella spotted figures moving in the cold on the other side of the closed glass door.

One of the figures was still pounding on the glass, demanding they open the door. Another looked like they were gesturing for someone carrying something heavy to join them.

A battering ram for the glass door?

Ella winced, but then as Brenner hurried forward to stall, she turned, twisted the handle to the door, and entered the interrogation room.

The door swung shut behind her with an ominous *click.*

And she found herself staring at her father where he sat behind the metal table. He frowned up at her, his eyes set in a mask.

She stared back, exhaled briefly, then locked the door behind her.

"Hello, Dad. I know you're mad, but," She stared at him. "I'm fifty percent sure you hired someone to kill the Longstreets."

CHAPTER 18

ELLA DIDN'T SIT ACROSS the metal table from her father, preferring to maintain her feet and pace slowly back and forth in front of the steel surface. Her father didn't speak, just watched her, his eyes narrowed—cold and cruel as ever.

Ella's fingers tapped nervously against her upper thigh, but her features were arranged into pleasant curiosity. She didn't bother trying to manipulate her old man. Everything she knew she'd learned from him.

"Hungry?" she said slowly. "Can I get you a drink?"

"You can get me out of here, Ella."

"I'd like to. Really. Just, I have a couple of questions."

"I answered your questions. You're going to regret this."

He said it so matter-of-factly, with such deep certainty that she had to pause long enough to remind herself he was only human. This was a mortal man just like anyone else, no matter what he pretended to be.

She said, "I'm trying to find mom."

Her mind filled with images of Lois Porter. The Queen of Nome. And she had enjoyed her rule as much as her husband. A dispassionate, critical woman. A woman who hadn't seen much in her daughters except pieces to be moved, tools to be used. No... No that was her father. For her mother? They'd just been props.

"Trying to find her? And so you harass her husband?"

"I want to know about the two men you sent to threaten Mr. Longstreet."

Silence.

She stared at him, and he stared back without blinking.

"What men?" he said.

"No—see, that was too late. A couple seconds too late. So you *did* send the men? I wasn't sure. Just trying to confirm."

Her father glanced towards the door. "I hear voices. Someone doesn't sound happy. Priscilla?" he asked, flashing a crocodile grin. "I always could rely on your sister."

"I don't know who is out there," Ella replied. A lie. Was Brenner right? She really did lie too much. But in this case, it was for a good cause.

"So what happened exactly?" Ella said.

"With what?"

"The two men you sent to threaten Mr. Longstreet."

"No threats. If I did send anyone, it would have been as a delegation. A business deal. I'm a businessman, not a mobster."

She stared at him. "That's impressive."

"What is?"

"That you can say that with a straight face."

"Now, now, Eleanor. Respect thy father and mother."

"What is that? Shakespeare?"

Her father actually grinned now. His eyes still burned with anger, but the look of amusement was genuine. "You always did have a spark, didn't you? I'm going to regret what I have to do."

"Have to do?"

He didn't reply, glancing into corners of the ceiling, searching for a camera.

She said, "So when you sent your gun thugs to propose to Mr. Longstreet, what happened?"

"A business deal was proposed, perhaps. But I don't know what happened."

"How come?"

"I never heard back from my delegation. Now, is that all? See—you could have just asked me back at the house. All of this unpleasantness wasn't worth it, was it?"

Now, Ella could hear the loud voices had entered the marshal's office. She could hear stomping footsteps. A table toppling. More shouting. Brenner was putting up a good fight, but she was on borrowed time.

And so she did the one thing that might calm tempers. She approached her father and uncuffed him.

He frowned, staring down at his wrists, massaging them. He looked up.

"This doesn't make us even."

"I'm not trying to get even, Dad. I'm trying to find Mom."

"You have a funny way of going about it. I'm the victim here."

"Maybe. Usually not, but maybe you got a turn this time."

Her father shook his head, standing slowly as if uncertain whether she might intervene. When she didn't, he threw his shoulders back, rolling them and letting out a sigh. He pushed the chair back with his heel, his bathrobe falling about him like bedsheets.

Ella said. "And what if I think you hired those two men to kill the Longstreets?"

"What two men?" he snapped.

"The ones found buried in the ice. Under the sea. The ones on the Revcot." She stared at him.

He just watched her, cold.

She considered the clues a moment longer. Then nodded. "Back at their house. One of the rooms is stripped. The carpet gone. The bookcase gone. Someone died in that room. Maybe *two* someones."

She spoke clearly, concisely, watching her father closely. It was a fishing trip. But one with evidence. "I know you, dad. Vince used to work for you. The idea that he'd get the Revcot?" She made a tutting sound. "Over you? No. And if he refused a *deal* with you?"

The image of the text message, before it was deleted, flashed through her mind.

"Equally no deal."

"What are you talking about?" he pressed his knuckles on his right hand against the metal table.

"You sent men to kill Vince and Janice," she said. "I'm guessing they didn't make it out of that house alive. The carpets ripped, the books removed. Blood everywhere, right?"

"What are you talking about?"

"What I don't understand is why no police report was made. How did the bodies end up on the Revcot? Was that Vince, or you?"

"You're stretching here, Ella. Let it go."

She shook her head. "I don't think so. If you sent gun thugs after Vince once over at the Revcot, then maybe you did it a second time. Where's Janice?"

"I don't know!"

"Where's mom?"

"You tell me!" he snarled. "How about Baron, hmm? Jones. I hear he had gold dust on his fingers. He's a thief. He probably killed Janice."

Ella hesitated. Gold dust on his fingers? Had the coroner been speaking to her father?

She shivered. Baron *was* a thief, she'd decided. Part of her wondered if Baron had helped her father find Janice, alone. Maybe Baron had been paid by Mr. Porter to keep tabs on the Longstreets, to mention when it was best to take another shot...

Or maybe she was still missing something.

"I'm at sixty percent," she said. "I know you hired men to kill Vince and Janice. And I think you did it again."

"Prove it! Or get out of my way!"

Suddenly a fist started pounding on the interrogation room door. "Open up, now, Ella! God dammit, open this door! Dad! Dad are you okay?"

Ella glanced back at the door she'd locked, wincing. She turned to look at the one-way mirror, staring at her reflection. A pretty, tired face with blonde hair stared back. The funny thing was, on the other side, the same face was likely looking straight at her. Priscilla's sea-shell earrings, the only thing that would have helped most to distinguish the two of them.

It had been a matter of great pride for Priscilla that she loved the ocean that Ella dreaded.

But Ella didn't reply, instead turning back towards her father. He nodded towards the locked door. "I think that's for you," he said, forcing himself to calm again.

"Where did they go to speak with Vince?" she replied.

"Come again?"

"You called it a delegation. Two gun thugs. But you say delegation."

"What makes you think there were two gun thugs?"

"Because they were found dead at the bottom of the sea. Someone was killed in Vince Longstreet's library."

"That's flimsy."

"It was until you hesitated after I asked you, dad."

"I think we've had quite enough questions for today."

Her father stepped towards the door, and Ella did something she rarely ever did. She stepped in front of him, blocking his path.

The tall, silver-haired man stared down at her, still smelling of sandalwood aftershave.

She didn't flinch. "I'm almost done," she said graciously, but her eyes were flint. "Where did you send your gun thugs, Dad?"

"I wouldn't characterize my employees in such a manner."

"Where?"

Her father stared at her, and for a moment, she wondered if he would lay hands on her. His eyes were narrowed—the anger there suggested he wanted nothing more than to hit her. But he also knew this town. Knew to think two moves ahead.

She watched the way her father's eyes darted towards the door behind her. Likely, he wasn't thinking about Chief Baker or his other daughter. But about Brenner Gunn.

The trailer park kid.

The one who had always stood up to his old man to protect his mother. She wondered if her father had heard what had happened to Vince after the man had laid hands on Ella.

"Brenner's doing well, isn't he?" her father said slowly. Nothing in his inflection, but she knew he meant it sarcastically. And she also knew it meant she was guessing right, his mind was on her ex. And specifically, on what Brenner might do—witnesses or not—if he thought that Jameson had laid hands on Ella.

And so instead of shoving past her, Jameson sighed and said softly. "My delegation went to find Vince at his inland mine. Finding nothing, and breaking nothing I should add, they went to speak with him at his home. I never heard back from them. Vince claims he never saw them."

Ella nodded slowly. "What do you think happened to them?"

"Mr. Longstreet suggested that someone had taken ten ounces from a safe of his. Which is why you should look into Baron Jones. Thieves are as good as highwaymen in this town, Ella. They'd kill for an ounce."

"So two of your men just vanished?"

Her father shrugged. "It's possible I made a mistake in hiring those two. I don't even remember their names."

"That's not true," said Ella, gently. "You remember everyone's names."

Her father smiled now. "A trait we share, isn't that right?"

Ella shrugged. And she stepped aside. Her father slipped past, gathering his sleeves. Priscilla was now pounding on the glass. There was a loud *crack!* And the window splintered. Spiderwebs extended across the glass.

Ella rolled her eyes. "It's bulletproof!" she shouted out.

Another *crack*. And another spiderweb over the glass. Ella shook her head in disbelief. Her sister had always been a control freak. It made sense, she supposed, that Priscilla would start *shooting* at the interrogation room just to have her way.

Her father didn't seem to mind. He was smiling now and reached the locked door to the interrogation room, flicking the lock from the inside and then pulling the door slowly open.

As he did, Ella said, "So you think your delegation stole from Vince and ran?"

Her father looked at her. "No. I think that's what Vince says. I don't know what happened to them." He turned now, frowning. "I don't think you know either. I think you're fishing."

Ella paused, then nodded. "Like I said, we found them both dead on the Revcot claim, buried in a paystreak."

He just sniffed, shrugged as if disinterested, then pushed through the door, stepping out into the hall.

A couple of police were waiting, already apologizing profusely. Brenner Gunn was speaking to Chief Baker off to the side. The two of them had been in high school together, but neither of them had much liked the other.

Brenner had always been the superior athlete, but he'd never made any of the teams. Baker's parents had paid for the gymnasium.

As Ella stepped out of the room, behind her father, certain he meant every word about making her pay for this offense, she felt a sudden blow against the side of her cheek. She reeled back with a yell, head hitting the metal door, pain blossoming up her face.

Priscilla Porter stood facing Ella, her face twisted into a sneer, her finger jammed towards Ella. Her wrist shook. Cilla never had been able to control that temper. Daddy's girl took on a whole new meaning with Ella's sister.

Brenner was shoving past Chief Baker now. "Get the hell out of my way, Matt!"

Baker tried to grab Brenner's arm and received an elbow.

Ella reached up, touching at her lip, pulling her fingers away to find blood. Priscilla stepped forward again, her eyes blazing, her finger curling to form a fist. "You ever come near my family again," Priscilla was saying, her voice quavering with emotion. "And I'll bury you under the ice, you dumb bitch!"

Mr. Porter glanced back at his daughters, his eyes laden with amusement. The two cops who'd been speaking to him were cursing, hastening over to help Matthias Baker as he fought with Brenner Gunn.

Chief Baker hit the ground with a dull thump. The second cop hit the ground a second later as Brenner threw him over his hip. The third cop, deciding on a wiser course of action, didn't come in close but scrambled for his weapon, pulling it to aim at Brenner. "Get on the ground! Get down, now!" the cop yelled.

But Brenner's own gun leapt into his hand faster than thought. He was so quick on the draw that Ella nearly missed it when she'd blinked from the pain in her cheek.

Pandemonium reigned in the marshal's office. Brenner was shouting. The cop with the raised gun bellowed back. Another figure—the stocky bodyguard from the wharf—was rushing into the marshal's office, moving from the direction of a parked Range Rover where he'd been keeping an eye on the vehicle. He hurdled the table with the teapot, cursing as his own gun leapt into his hand.

Priscilla was still screaming threats at Ella, Brenner wasn't saying a thing, his lips sealed now that he'd decided on a more violent course of action.

Ella was struggling to shake the dizziness from her head. She tried to step around Priscilla, calling out for everyone to calm down. But her twin sister blocked her path, shoving her back *hard*.

Finally, it was Chief Baker who shouted, "Enough! Cut it—guns down!" He had a deep, authoritative voice. The voice of a man built to lead. A voice and a demeanor he'd developed as the quarterback of the football team for three years.

Everyone glanced at him. Everyone except Brenner, who didn't seem to give two shits about Baker.

Ella didn't blame him. Baker had the voice for it, and the money for it, but he'd bought his position of authority as sure as she'd bought those hot-dog-smelling gas station gloves.

Still, the cop with the raised gun slowly lowered his weapon. The other cop, whom Brenner had knocked flat, was getting to his feet slowly, glaring at Mr. Gunn.

The stocky bodyguard who'd rushed over the table from the parked Range Rover was now at Priscilla's side, apologizing profusely for being late and standing behind her, his own gun pointed at the ground.

"Everyone who isn't law enforcement, get out!" Baker was yelling.

Mr. Porter cleared his throat. "Thank you, Matthias," he said softly, tapping the chief on the shoulder. "I've got it from here."

Chief Baker opened his mouth to issue another statement, paused, frowned, then sighed. It was like watching a balloon deflate. Baker turned slowly, muttered something, blinked a few times, then gestured for his cops to follow.

Both cops glanced at Porter, and only after he nodded did they follow Baker out into the main office space.

"Priscilla," said Mr. Porter, "We're leaving, dear."

Priscilla pointed a final time at Ella. "Watch your back!" she said, her voice cold. Then she shot a cold glance toward Brenner. "Hope you enjoy my sloppy seconds," she added.

Ella noticed something curious. Brenner was looking everywhere except in Priscilla's direction. As she marched past him, he refused to meet her gaze, to even acknowledge she was there. Strange.

Ella massaged her chin and her cheek a bit more, opening and closing her mouth to make sure nothing was broken.

Her father was the final figure standing in the room, once Priscilla and her bodyguard left the office. Jameson Porter looked at Brenner, sneered, then glanced at his daughter. "You will be hearing from me," he said quietly.

Ella didn't reply.

And then her father shrugged, turned and began to move away towards one of the waiting cars.

"We should arrest them, Dad," Priscilla was saying, making no effort to keep her voice low.

"With only three cops?" her father muttered. "Good luck," he said sarcastically. "The drunk would kill your husband before his gun left his holster. Now *move!*" His voice turned to a leonine growl.

It was enough to usher the rest of them from the office. Car doors slammed. The door to the marshal's office was left open.

Cold air swept through the office, into the back room where Ella and Brenner were still standing as if frozen in place.

"Well?" Brenner said at last, glancing at her and massaging his stomach with a wince. "Get what you needed?" His face was prickled with red from both blood rushing through his cheeks and the cold now swirling through the room.

Ella blinked a couple of times, still dabbing her fingers against her cheek. But then she nodded slowly. "My dad said Baron Jones was helping a crew of thieves."

"You believe him?"

"No. He's lying. He hired hitmen to kill Janice and Vince."

"Shit, really?"

"Yes."

"So your dad did it? He's the killer?"

Ella sighed. "I thought so. But... no. No he would've tried to arrest us, otherwise."

"What?"

"It... it's just who he is. He would've locked me up rather than walk away if he was scared. He didn't kill or abduct Janice."

"So... who did? Unless you're saying Janice killed Baron?"

"No. She didn't. She didn't kill any of them. But I think I know who did, and I think I know where they're hiding."

CHAPTER 19

"You're sure you know where it is?" Ella said carefully, her eyes fixed on the slopes ahead, the rough terrain on either side.

Brenner pulled the vehicle up the mountain slopes, moving slowly to avoid skidding on the ice.

The two of them sat tensed in the front of the SUV. Their retreat from the marshal's office had been a hurried one. After Brenner had locked up and engaged the security system as well as all the security cameras—in case Priscilla or any of her friends came back for a bit of vengeance—they'd set out immediately, only pausing to top off fuel.

Ella was shivering now, even with the windows closed at her request, the heat on full blast.

This was always the part of a case that most thrilled her. The moment of truth, on a precipice's edge. On one side, a potential tumble, a plummet. On the other, though? Vindication.

She was right. She knew she was right.

But...

It didn't all make sense. Not yet. Something was missing. But that was why they were here.

"It's there—see it?" Brenner was pointing through the windshield now.

She followed his indicating finger, and then she nodded in excitement. "I see it," she whispered.

And indeed, there it was, across the cold terrain, a dark outline of an inland mining operation. Most of the machines were either back in town for the winter or stored in the large warehouse visible as an outline under the moon.

The tall fence encircling the small operation was ratty, worn and rusted. Portions of the fence were missing.

"A bit of a janky business," Ella said carefully.

"Yeah, well, his inland stuff was never the money maker."

Ella stared into the dark, her eyes hurting from the cold. A small, wooden sign, painted white, displayed the name of the mining company. *Longstreet Ltd.*

She stared at the name as they navigated the treacherous trail, bouncing over thick rocks and along muddy, furrowed ground.

"So tell me again why you think they're involved?" Brenner said slowly.

"It's not *them*," Ella replied quickly. "No—just... wait—see that?"

Now it was her turn to point and they both tensed. Their car jerked to a sudden halt, going still. They'd kept the headlights dim, but now Brenner flicked them off, stranding them in the dark except for the small light flashing about inside the metal fence, near the old warehouse where the mining vehicles were currently stored, sheltered from the inclement weather.

Snow was beginning to fall again—large, puffy white flakes. The glow from the light inside the metal fence illuminated the tumbling flurry.

Ella was staring through the falling white, towards the light she'd spotted.

"Who is it?" said Brenner quietly. And there was a sudden *crack!*

And the windshield exploded. Bits of glass scattered inside the vehicle. Flurries of snow followed, swept in like water breaching a collapsed dam.

Brenner's hand leapt out nearly instantly, in a blinding reaction, pushing Ella's head down as he shouted, "Down—get down!"

Another *crack!* And a portion of the bumper was taken off by the high caliber fire.

"He's got a scoped rifle," Brenner whispered, keeping low, his voice shaking horribly.

"It's not *him*," Ella said sharply. "It's her."

"What, *who*? Janice?"

"Yes!"

Another gunshot. The tires exploded.

"That doesn't make any sense!" Brenner yelled. "Why would she cut the line to her own air?"

"Because! He didn't know it was her!"

"What?"

But Ella was now tugging at the door to the front seat. It had taken her some time to piece it together herself. She still didn't understand the full measure, which was why they'd come here.

But now, under fire, she was beginning to think she may have over-played her hand.

She tumbled out of the car, hitting the cold ground and letting out a gasp of pain, wincing and staring at the sky as she lay there, dazed.

Brenner crawled across the seats, using the open door to the SUV for cover. But the bullets weren't striking the door. Rather, they kept hitting the front of the car.

"She's crippling the vehicle," Brenner whispered softly. "Are you sure it's Janice?"

"I—I think so." Ella was shivering now, hunched as snow fell around them.

The inland mining operation was a couple of hours from town. Without a working vehicle, they were as good as dead out in the snow. They needed to reach the mine, but the sniper was keeping them pinned.

Brenner's gun was in his hands now. The six-foot-four soldier pressed a muscled shoulder against the door, keeping it from being caught by the wind and sent slamming into the two of them.

He inhaled slowly, then whispered, "I'm going to fire twice—then you need to shove the truck."

"What?"

"I left the brake off. Shove the truck—I'll hit the lights. It'll draw her fire." He paused, shooting her a look. "You're *sure* it's Janice?"

"I'll explain later. Yes—I'm sure. She didn't kill anyone, but she will. Trust me. It makes sense."

Brenner just shook his head in bewilderment, but the motion ceased as another bullet sparked off the door above his head. He cursed, ducking low, and gripping his weapon tightly.

He waited for a lull, then said, "Now! Now!"

He raised his weapon over the door and began firing shots back in the direction of the long gun. There was another lull in gunfire as Ella bolted from the cover of the door and hastened to the back of the truck. Then, following Brenner's instructions, she began to shove the vehicle, putting her small frame into it.

The truck began to roll forward. Brenner reached in, flicking on the headlights, then darted back.

He fired twice more, this time making it seem as if he were in the front seat of the truck, the muzzle flash illuminating over the steering wheel as he stretched his lengthy frame through the open door, his legs moving to follow the motion of the rolling car.

Then, after a final shot, the lights blaring, he yanked back, and tumbled to the ground, rolling in the mud and the snow and going suddenly still.

Ella had ducked low also, leaning over the embankment, peering down at a sharp drop, fifty feet below, and the thick boulders extending protruding portions upwards like spears of granite.

She shivered, staring at the fall, willing herself to refocus.

She willed her fear to the back of her mind, her skin prickling as she crawled along the muddy ground towards where Brenner lay, breathing in mud.

She reached his side, tapping a hand against his back, and whispering in his ear. "You good?"

He nodded.

"They firing at the truck?"

Ella whispered, "Looks like someone is moving to check it out."

The two of them crouched low on the muddy ground, alongside a thick furrow. A figure emerged in the headlights, a long-scoped rifle in her hands.

And Ella stared at a woman she recognized from the crime scene photos. Janice Longstreet. A tall, native-looking woman, with tan skin, dark hair pulled back and shaved at the sides. Severe, confident features. The woman glanced up the road, then back into the truck, muttering to herself and shaking her head.

She then called out. "Is that you, Porters? Cilla? Jameson?"

Ella tapped Brenner on the shoulder, and the two of them, keeping low, shuffled along the side of the road, moving through the mud, keeping low. A snowbank obscured them, hiding them from view as they moved in the snow, shifting along it and circling around towards the metal fence.

"Ella," whispered Brenner. "I think you're right. I think it's Janice."

Ella snorted in amusement but inhaled a flake of snow and nearly sneezed. The sky really was pouring frost across the ground. The snowflakes were now soft, downy and as big as her thumb.

Beautiful on a Christmas card but deadly for those caught in the elements... late at night, fifty miles from civilization.

Brenner began to aim, slowly, over the snow bank, towards the woman in front of the headlights. But as he did, Ella hissed, "Wait—don't. Look!"

She froze, figuratively.

The two of them stood poised, staring at the ground, and watched as a second figure emerged from behind the large warehouse. And he prodded a third person along in front of him. The man with the thick, reddish beard she instantly recognized as the lumberjack who'd assaulted her back at the yurt.

Vince Longstreet.

She stared and nodded. "Okay—I get it now."

"Mind cluing me in?" Brenner whispered. "Is that Vince?"

"You swore he wouldn't have killed his wife. Well—you were right." She kept her voice low, her face low too, only occasionally peering over the snowbank.

"I... why did he cut her line, then?"

"He was trying to kill her."

"What?"

"He was going to kill her. But then he realized who it was."

"I..." Brenner frowned.

Ella just shook her head. She was going to explain further, her voice still barely a whisper, waiting patiently for the Longstreets to turn and leave, but then she spotted the figure they had with them.

Her mother.

Lois still hadn't aged a day, and her features were as imperious as ever, with supermodel good looks, evident even in the rising blizzard, her face illuminated by the headlights of the perforated SUV. She stood tall, proud, but clearly scared. She was wearing a large coat, suggesting, at least, the Longstreets had some common decency.

"I don't get it," Brenner was repeating again. Then he cursed. "No clear shot. She's in the way."

Ella found her heart hammering, staring at her mother, grasped in the clutches of those two figures.

She wanted to shout out, wanted to run down the hill to the rescue.

As much as she didn't get along with Lois... it was still her damn mother.

At this thought, Ella winced. This place really was getting to her. She let out another puff of air and closed her eyes. The mist from her breath dusted the sky in streaks of gray, mingling with the snowflakes and mercifully disguised by the tumbling ice.

"Porter?" screamed Vince Longstreet. "I know it's you! Show your ass. Show it now!"

Gone was the screaming, desperate, whining voice of the man who'd wept at the crime scene. Now it seemed so obvious. Driving his truck over the ice, stumbling into the yurt.

The one place he hadn't looked for his wife was the place he *should* have.

Under the ice.

But Vince had been a diver too. Just not a very good one. Most of his time, she reasoned, would have been spent above the water, in the chair, keeping tabs on things. Except that one time.

The time, a year ago, they'd gone to speak to Dilahunty about the Revcot claim.

Yes... yes, it all made sense now.

Vince had intentionally fallen on Baron, intentionally contaminating the crime scene. He'd intentionally messed with things in the yurt, in order—perhaps—to pocket something they hadn't noticed. Or just to sow mayhem.

And then he'd put hands on Ella. Not because he'd thought she'd killed his wife. He'd known Janice was alive.

No... but rather because he'd been furious at the Porters... and with good reason.

Her father had sent gun thugs into their own home. Something must have happened. Something that meant Vince wasn't *able* to come clean about shooting the men in his own home. This was the part that hadn't clicked at first. Why not just call the police? If two men had broken into his home and he'd stabbed them, even if from behind and they'd been unarmed, he could easily have claimed self defense...

Except one thing.

The Revcot claim.

Vince Longstreet had been bidding on the Revcot; an investigation into a double stabbing would have been enough to nudge the owner of the Revcot to go with another bidder. Perhaps that was what her father had intended, after all. If they killed Longstreet, he won the bid. If Longstreet killed them, tarnishing his name and reputation in the eyes of a man like Dilahunty, especially if under suspicious circumstances—if the men's backs had been to him, unarmed, perhaps—then her father *still* won. Getting the bid as a reliable businessman rather than a gun-wielding, man-killing frontiersman.

It was exactly the sort of play her father would make.

But Vince had played the game too. He hadn't called the cops. He'd killed them in his home, though.

Yes... the missing carpet. The missing books.

But now, a new obstacle in front of her. Her mother at gunpoint. Janice still had the sniper, aiming it towards the truck and vaguely up the slopes of the mountain trails. But Vince kept his own handgun pointed directly at Lois' head.

"I'll count to five, Porter, and then I'll waste her. You know what I want! Give it to me, and this is all over!"

Ella shivered again, and she shot a panicked look at Brenner.

"No shot," he said. "She's right between us." Brenner began to move slowly along the muddy incline on the side of the road, using the snowbank for cover.

But Janice suddenly yelled, "Vince, there! See? Movement by the snowbank."

Brenner went stiff.

Ella was panting horribly now and occasionally wanding a hand in front of her face to help obscure the rising columns of steam. She cursed and shook her head.

"Four! Three!" Vince was screaming. "Priscilla? Not Baker, is it? Two!"

Ella was tense. If she emerged, they'd likely just shoot her. But if she didn't, Vince was going to shoot her mother. He'd said he would, and she believed him. He'd already killed three men, after all. The two gun thugs had been killed upstairs in the room without a carpet.

Vince was a thorough man, though. That much was clear. He hadn't just ripped up the carpet. Hadn't just bleached the ground. He'd also removed the white outlet faces, possibly stained with blood. And then he'd removed the books from the bookshelf, suggesting *that* was where the men had been searching in the Longstreet residence when Vince had come up behind them and stabbed them.

Then the carpet had been disposed of. The books too. Likely burned.

All of that had happened a year ago.

That was when Dilahunty had said the Longstreets started asking about the Revcot claim. Not specifically about mining it but about the topography. The why was obvious.

They'd needed someplace safe to bury the bodies.

But in a gold mining town where every piece of coast was overturned, every ounce of dirt panhandled, in a place known as the largest gold-pan in the world, they had to find a place to bury the bodies where *no one* would look.

And so they'd chosen the Revcot.

Things had gotten dicey from there… Ella was still piecing it together. Why had he killed Baron? Why had he cut the line to his wife's oxygen? Had he intended to kill Janice but changed his mind?

Had he—

"One!"

She cursed and reached a decision.

She emerged from behind the snowbank, standing upright and waving her hands above her head. "Don't shoot! It's me, Ella! Don't shoot!"

Chapter 20

"Don't shoot," Ella repeated. She met Janice's eyes, staring down the woman with the scoped rifle as she held up her badge. "I'm with the FBI—see. Look! You don't want to kill me. The FBI knows I'm here. They know it. If you shoot me, they'll come for you. So far we don't have you on anything except for kidnapping. Alright?"

The words sprang unbidden from her lips but were uttered desperately as she stood there, in the cold, occasionally wincing against the pattering snow. She spat ice from her tongue, wincing and taking slow steps forward. She made sure to hug the left side of the road, opposite where Brenner crouched in the nearby snowbank.

"Where's your gun!" snapped Vince, shaking Ella's mother and gesturing with his own pistol.

"Here—holstered!" Ella said, tapping at her waist. She then pulled it out, held it slowly and tossed it off the cliff.

"What the hell!" Vince yelled.

"Oh—sorry? Did you want me to keep it? I was just trying to disarm myself..." Ella spoke in a gracious, stuttering sort of way. A disarming way. She was just a little pixie. A small, pretty girl, ten years too late to be a cheerleader. She was no threat. Nothing to worry about. Just another pawn and a tool to be used. The less they thought of her, the better.

She smiled as she came towards the three figures illuminated by the steaming SUV's bright lights.

But as she drew nearer, as she kept her hands upraised, and as she breathed slowly in the snowy sky, she spotted her mother staring straight at her.

Ella hadn't tossed the gun for any reason but to keep Vince from counting the bullets. If he saw that she hadn't fired any, then he'd know that someone else was with her. But now, with the gun safely at the bottom of the gully, they wouldn't know she'd come with someone else.

"Where's your backup?" Vince snapped, eyeing the snowbank.

"Oh—umm, yeah. I was back there."

"You came alone?"

"Yes, but as I said, the FBI knows I'm here. You're being watched right now." She pointed up towards the sky, confidently, indicating a flight path with her finger—perfectly imaginary but enough to spark the fears of her would-be captors.

Vince looked up, frowning. Janice sneered. "Shut up. You're not FBI. I know you—you're Priscilla Porter."

But Vince shook his head. "She's a twin."

"What's that?"

Lois said now, "This is my other daughter, Janice. Let me introduce you," the woman said coldly. And even at gunpoint, even having been kidnapped from her own subdivision, her dog killed in front of her, Mrs. Porter looked like a woman in charge. Like the Queen of Nome. She said, "This is Eleanor. She hasn't been home for twelve years but was recently assigned to the FBI field office in Nome." Mrs. Porter continued without even hesitating, "If she says the FBI is watching, you'd better believe her."

Lois had always been good at going along with the family's lies.

"Shut up," Janice snapped again.

"How very eloquent," Lois sneered. "Any other phrases you learned at the bottom of the sea? Hmm?"

Vince shoved the woman before Janice could slap her. "God dammit," Vince said. "It's cold. Ella, you're coming with us. Janice, make sure no one follows then join me in the warehouse."

"What then, Vince?" Janice snapped.

"I'm thinking."

"Your thinking got us here!" Janice yelled.

"Dammit, I know!"

Ella cleared her throat. "I'm so sorry," she said. "Not to interrupt. But did you know it was your wife diving when you killed Baron and tried to kill her?" Ella pointed at Janice then at Vince, she smiled congenially.

Vince Longstreet scowled at her.

Janice's eyes flicked. Somewhere between pain and fear as well. A memory conjured, perhaps?

"Let me guess," Ella said slowly, standing under the falling snow. Out of the corner of her eye, she spotted movement by the snowbank as Brenner tried to circle towards a hole in the rusted fence. As he moved low and swift over muddy terrain, occasionally wincing and grasping at his right leg, Ella spoke louder, trying to focus all attention on her. "Vince, you thought someone was diving on the Revcot claim without your permission, is that right? Janice had gone with Baron, though. You knew they were directly on the sandbar where you buried those bodies of the gun thugs my father sent to your house."

"Vince," Janice said sharply. "They know. God dammit, Vince, they know everything!"

Lois was nodding. It was an impressive skill that Lois could both communicate approval of the Longstreets' fear while also expressing disapproval of the person causing it.

Ella said, "Janice didn't tell you she was diving, did she?"

Vince was scowling at his wife. "How does she know this?"

Janice just shook her head, shoving Ella forward. "Shut up!" she snapped again.

But Ella just nodded slowly. It made sense. It clicked into place. Vince Longstreet had buried the bodies on the Revcot land. And then, he'd seen a strange outfit *mining* on the Revcot in the exact location he'd buried the bodies. Scared that someone was going to discover what he'd done, he'd taken care of the problem.

He'd killed Baron, then gone to kill the diver, only to discover—almost too late—the diver was his wife.

"Wow... that must have been a rough conversation, huh?" Ella said, as she moved towards the warehouse, shivering but speaking louder. She'd lost sight of Brenner. "After trying to kill her, realizing who it was—did you apologize? Was that it? Janice didn't know where you buried the bodies... but she knew you had. She was in on it. She didn't want the bid for the Revcot to collapse. Dilahunty plays the role of an old-timer, but he's a newcomer after all. Comfortable with businessmen, not frontiersmen. My father would've gotten the claim if Dilahunty found out you'd killed those two men, even in self-defense."

"Just shut up already!" This time instead of a shove by a gloved hand, Ella felt something cold and metal jam against her spine, sending her stumbling forward.

She slipped in the snow, wincing.

Her mother glanced at her but didn't reach to help her up.

Vince Longstreet was shaking his head, cursing and pulling with grunts on the metal handle of the cold warehouse door. The large frame began to slowly slide open with each tugging motion. As it did, though, his voice shook in frustration. "Should've told me, Jan. We agreed we'd tell each other when we were mining!"

"I didn't know!" Janice yelled. "You didn't tell me where you god damn buried them! You should've told me!"

Vince sobbed, shaking his head, his beard swaying. Little flecks of frost stuck in his woolly facial hair. "I didn't know it was you, Jan... I swear I didn't." He turned now, his gun low, tears in his eyes.

Janice sighed, approaching her husband, shouldering her rifle. She leaned in, stroking his beard, her fingers curling and tugging at knots of red hair. "I know, honey. I know you didn't. You gave me a little scare is all. I forgive you."

She leaned in, her fingers wrapped through his beard and holding him tight under the ear as she pressed his lips to hers in a long and forceful kiss.

Lois was inching back away from the door and the two kissing, gun-totting gold miners. But then, Janice spotted the retreat. She instantly released her husband, spinning sharply. "Hey! Don't move!" she snapped, raising her weapon and pointing it at them.

Lois went stiff. Ella's hands remained raised.

And that's when two gunshots echoed behind them.

The first one took Janice in the neck. She stumbled back, blinking, opening her mouth, closing it, and then falling to the ground, bleeding in the snow.

The second shot hit Vince. But because he was standing so close to Lois, Brenner had aimed wide. The bullet clipped Vince along the shoulder, spinning him like a top.

But he recovered quickly, his own weapon rising. He fired twice as well.

The first bullet hit Lois Porter in the arm. The woman stumbled back, letting out a small, controlled sound like *oof*.

The second bullet was aimed in the direction of the shooter. By the looks of things, Brenner was on top of the fence, perched there, sitting with his legs thrown on either side.

As Vince fired back, though, Brenner dropped on the other side, into the mine, ducking behind a large fuel pump.

Vince was cursing and spitting. He crawled in the snow towards his wife. "Janice!" he was screaming. "No—no, GOD! JANICE!"

It was the same desperate pleading voice he'd used when faking back at the ice-mine. Now, though, the tears were real. The terror real.

He gripped at his wife, shaking horribly, his fingers coming away stained in red. Janice's eyes stared lifeless at the sky, open and accusing. Small snowflakes tumbled, settling on her cheeks. On her open eyes.

She didn't blink.

Ella was at her mother's side, trying to tug the woman to safety. But Vince was now cursing and spitting, enraged. He slammed into Ella, knocking her down, then he pointed his gun at her, firing again.

But this time, he was too slow on the draw. *Crack!* "OW!"

Brenner had shot Vince's gun from his hand before he'd managed to execute Ella. Now, the large, bearded man stumbled back, clutching his hand. Two of the fingers were bent horribly. Rapidly turning purple as blood swelled inside the skin. He tripped over his wife's body, weeping and cursing, and then retreated.

"Sorry, s-sorry Janice!" He slipped through the opening in the warehouse doors, disappearing in the dark and leaving his wife dead on the ground.

Ella, breathing heavily, shoulders pressed to the snow, wet creeping up her spine, breathed heavily. And then she turned sharply, facing her mother and quickly applying pressure to the wound in Lois' arm. "Press this here," she snapped, using the woman's scarf as a tourniquet.

But Lois was already busily doing it herself. She didn't make a peep. Didn't hiss in pain. Just, pale-faced, went about her business, wrapping her arm tight, and ignoring Ella completely.

Lois and Ella both regained their feet. As Ella tried to help her mother, though, Lois shoved her hand away.

Ella began to speak, but just then, there was a grumble. A roar.

And then a bright light.

Ella's eyes widened in horror. She had only a second to fling herself into her mother, knocking Lois to the side as a snowmobile burst from inside the warehouse's open sliding door.

The sleek, black vehicle hurtled forward. Vince was sitting on it, still openly weeping, skidding to avoid his wife's corpse. He'd been aiming for Lois, but missed as Ella slammed her mother aside.

A split second to make a decision. Ella knew it was foolish. But again, her mother's tone—her mother's complete lack of warmth, of gratitude. All of it. Priscilla, Chief Baker. It tugged at her stomach. The same way the anxiety had under the ice when she'd stayed down for too long.

A surge of adrenaline. A surge of *need* to do something... wild.

And so Ella reached out—even as she shoved her mother, she snatched at the speeding snowmobile. Grabbing at Vince.

Her arm nearly jolted from its socket, but she held on, draped across his form. She kicked twice as he picked up speed, but he was strong.

A thrill of excitement as the snowmobile sped rapidly forward, but she wasn't seated properly. Instead, she kicked, struggling, half draped over the damn thing.

"Get off!" Vince screamed, trying to pull at her. But she was in an awkward position now, half draped over his lap, holding onto his knees, tight. Trying to jerk back and forth.

She realized how stupid she must have looked, but they were only going faster. She refused to let go. And if she had, now, at this speed, it would've meant collision.

Instead of trying to pull her off now, Vince tried to readjust where she was trying to twist his knee, to knock him off the seat. He yanked her frail form, pushing her away from his knee, along the space between his seat and the handlebars. She desperately tried to fight, but his powerful grip tightened on her neck, squeezing threateningly.

All the while, they picked up speed, racing over ice and snow, gliding along the trail, towards the opening in the mine's gated entrance. The SUV's headlights were dimming now.

But the snowmobile raced for it.

Two gunshots. But Brenner was aiming for the machine, not the driver, fearful of hitting Ella. Ella tried to shout, but a hand covered her lips. Shit. She'd made the wrong call—but she simply hadn't been willing to let him get away. The danger, the terror of the moment seemed to *melt* the anger stored in her gut. And another emotion arose, but even this, the humiliation of helplessness—especially since she'd tossed her gun—was short-lived.

The terror of having her face towards the ground, inches above jutting stones and thick clumps of ice, was enough to force her to pay attention to her more immediate struggle.

Ella conserved her breath, and now—instead of screaming—her abdominal muscles clenched as she jerked up, trying to lift herself.

Her face narrowly avoided a boulder slashing towards her. She was still bent over the machine, face down, her cheek grazing Longstreet's leg where he gripped the side of the snowmobile like some horseman on a favorite stallion.

The engine grumbled and shook, reverberating in her ears where she lay. She tried to rise again, but this time, he shoved her head down. They skidded with the motion as he momentarily lifted his grip from the handlebars.

He cursed, and Ella shouted.

They nearly careened into a thick, stony boulder. But he redirected just in time, sparing them the deadly collision.

She could feel him shaking, weeping where he leaned over her like some ghoul, holding her in place with his elbows, with his knees. She was draped over the seat in front of him while he simultaneously attempted to navigate the machine across the dangerous incline, up the mountain roads.

She struggled desperately to free herself, snatching at his boot, and tugging at the hem of his pants. She managed to disentangle his shoelaces, and he yelled, beating her across the back of the head.

She went still, wincing, her head ringing as pain lanced through her skull.

They were picking up speed, now, hastening further and further up the mountain slopes. As she lay helpless, draped over the snowmobile, her mind protested the inevitable fate awaiting her. She didn't have a weapon. He was much larger than her.

The best chance she had was for both of them to be knocked clean of their machine. But it would be painful.

She stared at where his untied laces dangled down. She wondered if she could tie the laces to the machine's footguard and then try and throw herself the other way. He'd compensate, as he'd been doing, forcing her back in position.

But the motion would jerk his leg, would unbalance the machine.

And at these speeds, they'd careen off the road.

She shivered, frozen in indecision.

But she had to make a choice. The further they went, the worse it would became. She was going to suffer injuries—that much was clear. Horrific injuries.

She would need to be rushed to a hospital. Same as her mother.

She had a sinking sensation this wasn't going to end well. She had to weigh her options... would Vince Longstreet let her live if he took her to a second location?

After what had happened to his wife?

He'd likely torture her instead. It all lined up now. She breathed heavily, her chest in pain, her abdomen pressed against the seat.

VL had texted *no deal.*

Her father had then sent gunmen to get what he'd wanted. Probably something to do with the Revcot. And then Vince had killed them both and buried them on the same claim.

Vince had also once been her father's secretary as she'd told Brenner earlier. That was how he would've known Mrs. Porter's schedule. The missing camera in the back. The way she'd walk her dog.

Brenner had been right. Vince *hadn't* killed Janice. But he'd been wrong about one thing.

Men like Vince, men like her father. They loved their wives. Deeply, even. But there was something they loved more.

And it glistened.

The missing pages from the journal. Vince had burned those, the same as he'd likely burned the books from his upstairs room. Payment records to employees...

One of his employees had been Baron.

What if the payments had included something else... something like a bribe? What if Baron had helped Vince bury those bodies?

She didn't think she'd ever know for sure.

But it was this last part that made up her mind.

Vince was willing to kill a trusted employee to keep his secrets. Was willing to kill an unknown diver for the same thing, until he'd found out it was his wife.

For someone he hated? Someone who was the daughter of the man who'd—in a way—started all of this by sending thugs to Vince's own home?

The person who'd brought the gunman who'd killed his wife?

There'd be no mercy.

He'd kidnapped Lois Porter, after all. An insurance against Jameson Porter's encroachment on the Revcot, and certainly at least some amount of revenge.

No... No, she had to take action.

And it was going to hurt.

She reached out with shaking fingers, her whole body vibrating from the engine's rattle. She reached for the dangling shoe strings, which were soaked now from where they flicked across the icy ground, and tied them around the metal footrest, moving hurriedly.

They were speeding further up the mountain, further and further from the mine.

The more distance they traveled, the less chance Brenner would have of finding her injured body. She summoned her will. It would hurt, but she didn't care. Bones would break. She hissed. But she didn't care.

It was a roll of dice.

But so were many things.

A surge of adrenaline, and then she yanked to the side, determined to topple the snowmobile and send them careening off the road.

CHAPTER 21

Brenner had dropped to Lois' side, double-checking she was all right. The woman had clasped a bandage made from a scarf around her bleeding arm. She recoiled from his touch, scowling at him as if he was somehow doing something improper.

Crazy old bat.

He didn't have time for this. Double-checking the ungrateful Queen of Nome was still breathing, he snatched the scoped rifle from the ground, surged to his feet, and released a long, pent-up breath.

He raised the weapon, feeling the familiar touch of the stock against his shoulder, the scope to his eye. The barrel, long and smooth; his hand under, cupping the faux wooden grip.

It felt like a homecoming.

He exhaled slowly, emptying his lungs, bracing his leg against the rusted metal gate. He watched the snowmobile speeding away, faster, faster. Veering up the mountain incline.

He tensed—if he waited too long, the vehicle would reach deadly speeds.

He sighted through the scope, adjusted—then tore the thing off—he didn't trust the sights had been adjusted.

He used the iron sights instead. The scope at his feet, in the snow.

"Boy," said Lois, tottering. "Hey—you. Come here, help me." Her voice was strong, dispassionate, but he spotted fear in her eyes as she bled. Typical Porter—the only way she knew to deal with anxiety was to exert control. But Brenner had seen wounds like hers before. Nothing major hit. Her daughter, on the other hand?

Lois was trying to remain straight-postured, her expression one of courage. But there was a faint sneer on the woman's face when she glanced at Janice's corpse.

Brenner ignored her, watching as the snowmobile lifted over the incline, beginning to dip. It was about a quarter mile away.

Without a scope.

His finger tensed, relaxed, and he squeezed.

Bang!

Vince flew over the front of the seat. Ella, who'd been draped across the snowmobile, her fingers busy with something near Vince's foot, suddenly jolted upright. The snowmobile veered sharply. Ella yelled—he could just hear her over the sound of the padding snow.

His heart pounded, and for a moment, he saw something other than Ella.

A small, cherubic smile. Gleaming eyes. A child's face, laughing. "Daddy!"

A tear traced down the inside of his cheek. He puffed air, staring at where the snowmobile had toppled. Ella had only held on for a few brief moments, gunning the machine into a bank of snow, cushioning the collision.

Vince lay motionless on the side of the mountain, hit square between the shoulder blades.

Brenner closed his eyes, inhaling through his nose, exhaling deeply.

He felt his heart pound rapidly. And in his mind's eye, he pictured *her*. *Daddy!* He'd often said the happiest time of his life had been the five years in the Navy.

But that wasn't strictly true.

There had been another period of life.

It had ended far too quickly.

In fact, it had been the real reason for leaving the Navy. The real reason he'd come back home.

But fate had taken that from him too.

Anything he ever cared for, like his mother, like *her,* it was always taken.

And so he stared at where the snowmobile had crashed in the embankment. Where Ella had careened into the frost, certain he'd made a mistake. Certain he'd left it too late. Perhaps he shouldn't have even taken the shot, preferring to leave her to Vince's mercies.

She was dead.

Like everyone else.

He knew it in his bones.

"Have I stopped the bleeding?" Lois said, the tall woman's voice shaking.

Brenner glanced over, did a double take, impressed. She'd managed to bind her own arm, her fingers trembling and stained red.

He blinked, his mind flashing with rage, with pain. She was shot. Cut her a break. She was shot. Help her.

But he stared at Lois, and all he could remember were the snide glances. The hatred. The demands that he leave their daughter alone. All he could remember was Priscilla. His horrible mistake.

He stared at her, sightless, and looked back towards the snowy cliff again. Everything felt numb.

And then movement. A figure sat up, cushioned by the snow. Moving slowly, tenderly pressing at her thin arms.

Ella doubled over, gripping the snowmobile for support.

Alive.

Very much alive.

A spark in his chest.

It was like a flame to fuel.

He tossed the rifle to the side and broke into a dead sprint, racing up the mountain slope, hurtling towards where she stood outlined against the impression in the snow.

As he ran, flakes continued to tumble thick and fast, obscuring the night, obscuring the sky and obscuring his vision. But he sprinted on regardless, slipping on mud, skidding on ice, but panting rapidly—his right leg aching—as he rushed to preserve the single burning ember.

The only sparking coal remaining in this desolate place.

CHAPTER 22

Ella winced, touching gingerly at her cheek with gloved fingers. Her shoulder ached, and when she moved, the cast shifted across her chest.

Brenner stared at her, across the small hospital clinic's streaked, tiled floors. "You look awful," he said.

She smiled and chuckled but held back the laughter. Her ribs hurt too much. In fact, everything hurt too much.

A nurse was watching the two of them curiously, occasionally peeking over a clipboard and pretending she wasn't eavesdropping. The clinic was used mostly by fishermen—far enough from town and close enough to the docks to allow for sparse and occasional foot traffic.

It was the place Brenner had brought her and her mother, the three of them on the snowmobile he'd captured from Vince. Now, police were scouring the mining site for the bodies.

Ella shivered at the thought.

Bodies.

Vince and Janice. Now just *bodies.*

She glanced at Brenner. His eyes kept drooping. And as she glanced out the window overlooking the cold, Bering sea, she spotted sunlight high in the sky, warming the frozen ground, but only a little. A true thaw was still off in the distance.

This was only a glimmer of light. A glimpse of warmth. Not yet the full thing. But a taste of what was to come.

Ella glanced back at Brenner where he leaned forward in the hospital waiting room chair. The plastic seat creaked under him, and his eyes drooped further. He jolted up suddenly. "What?"

She smiled now, shaking her head. "You really stayed up all night?"

He shivered, swallowed and nodded. "Hell yeah. Got your mom here. Got you here. Had to go back and help the cops find the corpses." He wrinkled his nose. "Chief Baker was not thrilled about that call, let me tell you. Kept talking about assaulting an officer."

"Well... You did kind of assault him."

"Was a love tap. Well... a tap."

Ella shook her head, sighing. She didn't want to talk about Chief Baker. Or Priscilla, or any of the Porters. Her father would make good on his promise to come after her. That much was obvious. Her sister would inevitably get her revenge—she always did.

And the police in Nome? She'd already made an enemy of their chief.

Hardly an impressive start.

She winced, wondering how she would frame the report back to Quantico. Only a few months. That was the goal, wasn't it?

Only a few months and she'd get out of this place.

She sighed, leaning back, head bumping against the plaster wall. "Thanks, Brenner."

He was dozing off again, and she let him. She watched as he slumped in his chair, exhaustion taking its toll. She smiled at him, his eyelids fluttering closed again, his handsome features caught by the sunlight through the open window. A strong chin, tangled blonde hair slicked back except for a few strands falling free. Sharp cheekbones and perfectly symmetrical lips. A strong nose...

She shook her head, wincing again. She glanced at the nurse. "I thought the arm wasn't broken?"

The nurse clicked her tongue, pretending she had only just noticed she was being addressed. "What was that, honey?"

"The arm," Ella said. "I was told it wasn't broken."

"No—no. The cast is just to make sure it stays unbroken. A bad sprain. Could've pulled your shoulder out. And the rest of you..." The nurse clicked her tongue. She glanced at the man half slumped over. "He didn't do this to you, did he, honey?"

Ella quickly shook her head, her eyes flashing. "No, ma'am."

The nurse paused, staring at her for a moment. She then raised a pen, pointing. "Do I know you?"

Ella quickly stared at the ground, giving a noncommittal shrug. She cleared her throat. "Say, do you know where the other woman is?"

"Oh—the one who was shot? Honey, this is a dockside clinic. We deal with busted legs and splinters and the clap. Not gunshots. We had to send her to the hospital. Only twenty minutes from here—I can give you the address if you—"

"No, that's fine! That's fine." Ella quickly shook her head, forcing a quick smile. "Just—is she going to be alright?"

The nurse shook her head, but said, "Probably. I don't know, though. You'll have to talk to her attending. But from what I heard, she'll be fine." Then, she dropped her voice to a conspiratorial whisper. "Do you know who that *was*, though?"

"Who?" Ella said innocently.

"Lois Porter herself!"

Ella just kept smiling.

"OH, darling, you must be new around her. Lois Porter is the wife of Jameson Porter—those two are as rich as God."

Ella frowned. "They're not," she said reflexively. The idea of comparing her parents to deities only soured her mouth.

"Oh, well, maybe not. But you should see if there's a reward for bringing her in. What happened, though?" The nurse said, suddenly excited, as if realizing she had an all-access, behind-the-scenes look into the lifestyles of the rich and famous.

But Ella just winced, pretending as if she hadn't heard and leaned back. "Anything for the pain?" she asked.

The nurse looked momentarily disappointed but then sighed and nodded. She held up a finger, tossed her dark curls to the side and then hastened back towards a medicine cabinet against the far wall. A thick, brass padlock secured the doors to the cabinet, and a small key emerged from a ring attached to a strap by the lady's waist. She hummed to herself as she searched for the appropriate key.

Ella took this opportunity to rise to her feet, still grimacing, and kick at Brenner's shoes.

He blinked awake, staring up and wincing.

She held a finger to her lips and nodded towards the door with urgent gestures. Brenner, always one for subtlety said, "What?"

She glared at him, eyes widening.

"Oh, hey, honey—here's your pain meds!"

"Don't I need a prescription for those?" Ella shot back.

The nurse look scandalized. "Do you want them or not?"

"No—sorry. We have to get going." She kicked Brenner in the shoe again for good measure.

He pushed to his feet, yawning as he did, but then he helped lead her out of the small, dockside clinic. Stepping through the greasy, sliding doors, they were confronted with the odor of cold fish. In the distance, she spotted a crabbing vessel heading out to sea to lay traps or perhaps to plot a route when the next season came.

She turned away and, with Brenner's help, limped towards their waiting vehicle. No longer the SUV which had been totaled by sniper-fire.

Now they squeezed into a tiny, bright green Buick. It smelled like an ashtray and had two yellow, foam dice dangling from the rearview mirror.

"Sorry about the smell," Brenner muttered, gunning the engine and slowly pulling out of the parking lot. "My uncle doesn't use it much anymore except to escape to the garage when my aunt is yelling at him."

Ella gave a quick shake of her head. "Totally fine. No problem. Thanks, Brenner. I mean it."

As she said it, her phone vibrated. She glanced down, staring. Another text from the same unknown number. *We need to talk.*

She hesitated, frowning.

"Everything okay?" Brenner said.

"Yeah… fine. Can you take me back to the motel?"

"Sure—which one was it again?"

"Cheap and Easy."

He snorted.

She frowned. "You just wanted me to say the name."

He shrugged, already driving in the correct direction. As they picked up speed, Ella texted back. *Who are you?*

No reply.

A slow chill spread up her spine.

***

She sat alone on the bed of the motel. She hadn't mustered the courage to ask for a new one. She hadn't wanted to rock the boat.

So she'd asked Brenner to do it.

Cowardly? Perhaps.

He sure had thought so. He'd snorted and walked away, without fulfilling her request.

And so she sat alone in the motel room that smelled vaguely of the latrine. The bed itself was lumpy in portions and far too soft in others.

In addition, it made that delightful, croaking, squeaking sound of rusted springs. The only liquids around to rust springs in a motel bed were *never* the good variety.

Wrinkling her nose, Ella moved to one of the kitchen chairs, wincing as she did, hobbling a bit.

And then she settled in the seat, placing her empty holster on the table. Gunn had promised to get her a new firearm. She didn't want to report the weapon missing on her first day. That would wait.

She sighed, though, staring at her phone.

The number hadn't replied back.

Who are you?

Then radio silence.

She frowned, her brow flickering. She considered all the options. Each one stranger than the next. Not Brenner. He'd been in the car with her. Not her family, she thought. They would have been far crueler with it.

Then who?

Who else did she know in Nome?

Or was it someone from back at Quantico playing games with her?

She bit her lip in frustration, considering the possibilities.

She sat in the dank, dusky motel room, frowning.

And then the phone began to vibrate, buzzing against the table. It emitted a rattling sound. *Bzzz. Bzzz.*

She stared as her phone began to inch, crawling towards the edge of the table. Last minute, she realized she couldn't reach out to catch it with her right hand because of the cast. She cursed, using her left—but missed.

She sprained a thumb against the table, cursing, and stared at the ground where the phone continued to buzz ominously.

Wincing, bending over, trying to retrieve the thing, she dropped it twice. Her back ached too.

At last, feeling very uncouth, she bent at the waist, groaning as she did.

The phone went silent.

Shit, dammit. She thought. Out loud she said, "Oh dear."

She picked up the phone just as it started to buzz again. A flare of frustration, but this time she snagged it. She answered.

"Hello?"

Her voice felt small, hollow in her own ears. Perhaps it was simply the damp acoustics of the motel room.

She turned away from the heating unit, which occasionally rattled as it blew into the small space. She gripped the phone tightly, her fingers numb—her thumb aching from where it had jammed against the table.

She heard nothing on the other end. She frowned, glancing at the screen to make sure she hadn't accidentally disconnected. She checked nothing was muted. Only then, as she lifted the phone to her ear once more, did she hear a faint, rattling breath.

She stiffened.

"Hello? Who is this?" she said, slowly.

Then the voice replied. It sounded like the voice of an old-fashioned librarian. A cultured, sophisticated voice, but with no auspices. A voice intentionally attempting to keep quiet, calm—to suppress any sudden outbursts of emotion. It was a monotone voice. But not in a boring, droning sort of way, but more like a voice with the confidence of choosing an intonation and sticking to it.

A voice she certainly recognized.

Except, the last time she'd heard it had been in the back seat of a police vehicle. The man had been in cuffs.

Until she'd let him go.

"Hello, Agent Porter," said the Graveyard Killer. "I hope I'm catching you at an appropriate time. I can call back later, if you'd like."

She stared, frozen in place, her own mouth sealed tight. Her eyes bugged. "H-how did you get my number?" she said, exhaling slowly.

"A friend."

"You... you say that a lot. You called yourself my friend. We're not friends, sir."

A soft, wheezing sound. It took her a second to realize he was chuckling. "You have done more for me, Agent Porter, than most of my friends ever have. You may not see yourself as my friend, but I am most certainly yours."

She had risen to her feet.

She hadn't even realized she'd risen.

She blinked, disoriented.

"Why are you calling me?" she said, her voice as cold as Brenner's had been when they'd first met yesterday morning.

"To thank you, in part. Not everyone would have done what you did."

"I don't need your thanks!" Ella said. "Don't call me here. It isn't safe."

"Should I come see you, then?"

"What? No!" Ella, suddenly aware of how loud she had said it, glanced at the window, terrified it was open. But no—the window was closed. The door locked. A sudden paranoia descended on her though. She was in Nome. This was her family's home.

Anyone could be listening. *Anyone.*

"Listen to me carefully," Ella said. "Never call me again."

A chuckle. "That's not going to happen."

She blinked. "What?"

"I'm not going to stop. In fact, I'm coming to visit you, Ella Porter. I hear you've been reassigned."

"How do you know that?" she demanded. "I'm not confirming or denying it, by the way."

"You don't have to. I'm looking at a copy of your assignment right now." He whistled. "A long way to Nome. But you're worth it. We need to speak in person."

"No, we don't," she said, and she hated that her voice sounded like it was pleading now. "We said what was needed the last time we met. We don't need to say anything else. Let it go!"

A wheezing laugh. "I can't do that, Ella. I wish I could, but I can't. We have to talk."

"Why do we have to?"

"Because I have more work to do."

She stood frozen to the floor now, ice crawling up her spine. She hadn't known if it had been a mistake. At the time, it had seemed like the best option. The only option. No one else would have understood. But it had made sense then.

Now...

Now she was wondering if she'd made a horrible error.

"You promised not to call me. You promised to leave me alone!" she yelled.

"I promised to continue my work. And you are instrumental to that, Ella Porter."

He'd killed seventeen already. Seventeen bodies left in graveyards all across the lower-forty eight. She had reason to believe he'd killed more but couldn't prove it and hadn't confirmed it.

And she'd let him go.

She hissed. "You can't come see me. I will arrest you the moment I see you."

A pause, a deep breath. "A risk I'm willing to take. You're too valuable to my mission. I'll see you soon, Ms. Porter. Have a lovely, sunny day."

And then he hung up.

And Ella stood in place. She closed her eyes then opened them again. But it wasn't a dream—wasn't a nightmare.

The call was real.

It was all too much. Just too damn much. She bent over hyperventilating. Her shoulder aching. Her ribs protesting in pain. But she couldn't help it. Her shoulders shook, her breath came in huffing gasps as she sobbed at the ground.

The exhaustion, the pain, the helplessness, all descended on her like a flock of vultures.

"I didn't have a choice," she whispered at the ground. "I—I had to!"

But the words sounded hollow.

No one would understand.

No one would believe her.

And so she bent double, sobbing at the ground in the small, dank motel room in a town she'd never wanted to see again.

And now she was doubly cursed. Not just the town, but a *man* she never wanted to see again. He was coming to visit.

The man who'd ruined her career was coming to see her.

A serial killer was coming to Nome.

GIRL IN THE STORM

A blizzard is coming, and a murderer known as the Mocking-bird stalks the snow.

Seven teenagers went into the mountains on a camping trip. Two days later, their parents lost contact.

And now a young woman's body is found tied to a tree. The campsite was destroyed, and the others are all missing. But rumors abound, and a folktale resurrects—legends say there's a wildman in the mountains known as the Mockingbird who mimics the voices of those he kills.

In the small, gold-mining town of Nome, FBI Agent Ella Porter is called in to hunt the killer in the mountains and to discover what happened to the other campers.

Meanwhile, Ella's father wants revenge against his daughter, and a serial killer from Ella's past—the man who cost her everything—is on his way to Nome.

OTHER BOOKS BY GEORGIA WAGNER

SHE DIES TONIGHT

The skeletons in her closet are twitching...Genius chessmaster and FBI consultant Artemis Blythe swore she'd never return to the misty Cascade Mountains.

Her father—a notorious serial killer, responsible for the deaths of seven women—is now imprisoned, in no small part due to a clue she provided nearly fifteen years ago.

And now her father wants his vengeance.

A new serial killer is hunting the wealthy and the elite in the town of Pinelake. Artemis' father claims he knows the identity of the killer, but he'll only tell daughter dearest. Against her will, she finds herself forced back to her old stomping grounds.

Once known as a child chess prodigy, now the locals only think of her as 'The Ghostkiller's' daughter.

In the face of a shamed family name and a brother involved with the Seattle mob, Artemis endeavors to use her tactical genius to solve the baffling case.

Hunting a murderer who strikes without a trace, if she fails, the next skeleton in her closet will be her own.

ALSO BY GEORGIA WAGNER

THE RIVER'S SECRET

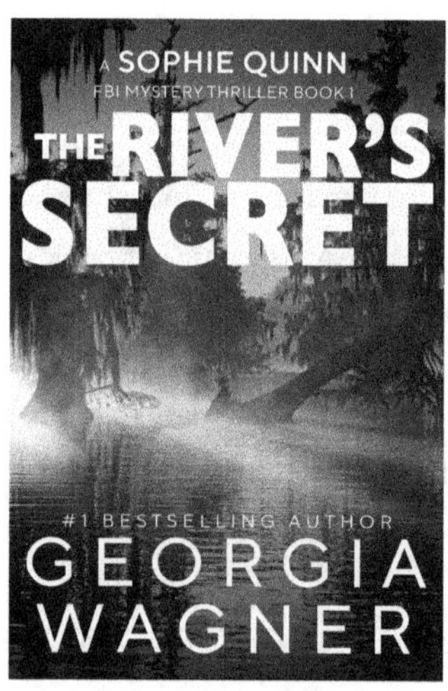

A cold knife, a brutal laugh. Then the odds-defying escape.

Once a hypnotist with her own TV show, now, Sophie Quinn works as a full-time consultant for the FBI. Everything changed six years ago. She can still remember that horrible night. Slated to be the River Killer's tenth victim, she managed to slip her bindings and barely escape where so many others failed. Her sister wasn't so lucky.

And now the killer is back.

Two PHDs later, she's now a rising star at the FBI. Her photographic memory helps solve crimes, but also helps her to never forget. She saw the River Killer's tattoo. She knows what he sounds like. And now, ten years later, he's active again.

Sophie Quinn heads back home to the swamps of Louisiana, along the Mississippi River, intent on evening the score and finding the man who killed her sister. It's been six years since she's been home, though. Broken relationships and shattered dreams exist among the bayous, the rivers, the waterways and swamps of Louisiana; can Sophie find her way home again? Or will she be the River Killer's next victim to float downstream?

WANT TO KNOW MORE?

Greenfield press is the brainchild of bestselling author Steve Higgs. He specializes in writing fast paced adventurous mystery and urban fantasy with a humorous lilt. Having made his money publishing his own work, Steve went looking for a few 'special' authors whose work he believed in.

Georgia Wagner was the first of those, but to find out more and to be the first to hear about new releases and what is coming next, you can join the Facebook group by copying the following link into your browser - www.facebook.com/GreenfieldPress.

GREENFIELD
PRESS

ABOUT THE AUTHOR

GEORGIA WAGNER WORKED AS a ghost writer for many, many years before finally taking the plunge into self-publishing. Location and character are two big factors for Georgia, and getting those right allows the story to flow seamlessly onto the page. And flow it does, because Georgia is so prolific a new term is required to describe the rate at which nerve-tingling stories find their way into print.

When not found attached to a laptop, Georgia likes spending time in local arboretums, among the trees and ponds. An avid cultivator of orchids, begonias, and all things floral, Georgia also has a strong penchant for art, paintings, and sculptures. A many-decades long passion for mystery novels and years of chess tournament experience makes Georgia the perfect person to pen the series.

www.ingramcontent.com/pod-product-compliance
Lightning Source LLC
Chambersburg PA
CBHW070625170726
48291CB00003B/886